kiniro
mosaic
7
Yui Hara

CHARACTERS

SHINOBU OOMIYA
Little Miss Prim?
KAREN KUJOU
Little Miss Impulsive ♪
YOUKO INOKUMA
Little Miss Enthusiastic!
AYA KOMICHI
Little Miss Bashful...
ALICE CARTELET
Little Miss Hardworking!

SUNDAY
RESTAURANT MATSUBARA
Restaurant Matsubara
カランカラーン
TING TING
WELCOME!
HUH?
キョロ GLANCE
キョロ GLANCE
HI, AYA-CHAN!
!!
ドキィ
AH!
HONOKA ...!

AHHHH...
ふあああん
SMILE OF RELIEF WHEN YOU FIND A FRIEND
WHAT A COINCIDENCE!!
UM...
I LIVE HERE...

IS IT JUST YOU TODAY?
THIS WAY, PLEASE.
ACTUALLY, WE'RE ALL MEETING UP. I GOT HERE TOO EARLY...

I'LL TAKE A COFFEE. BLACK.
NO SUGAR?
NATURALLY!
THAT SUDDEN CONFIDENCE!

HOW TO BECOME A POISED WOMAN
SLIP

WOW...

GROSS!
SPURT
ごふっ

THREE MINUTES LATER
YOUKO!
WHERE ARE YOU!? HURRY UP AND GET HERE!!
WELCOME!
WHISPER
ボソ
WHISPER
ボソ

WAIT, ISN'T THIS MATSUBARA-SAN'S FAMILY'S RESTAURANT ...!?
THIS IS WHERE YOU WANTED TO GO?
THAT'S RIGHT!
SENSEI...

WE'LL TAKE TWO IMPOSSIBLE PARFAITS.
NO!
WE SHOULD AT LEAST SHARE IT, RIGHT!?

OH YEAH. CAN I USE THE COUPON I GOT LAST TIME?
HEY! THIS IS EMBAR-RASSING IN FRONT OF A STUDENT ...!
カラン
DING
カラン
DING
くすくす
GIGGLE
GIGGLE

WHAAA—?
HEY, HONOKA! YOU HELPIN' OUT?
YOUKO-CHAN!
AYA-CHAN'S WAITING FOR YOU.
WHEEZE
ぜー
WHEEZE
ぜー

YOU'RE LATE!!
OH! HONOKA!
WHAAAT? BUT I EVEN RAN HERE. YOU'RE CRAZY!
WELCOME!

SORRY WE'RE LATE!
AFTER SHE SAID THEY WERE ALL MEETING UP...
...I ASSUMED KAREN-CHAN WOULD BE COMING TOO...

NOT TODAY, I GUESS.
TAKE THIS TO TABLE FIVE, PLEASE.
TOO BAD...
GOT ...

...IT...
CLATTER
がっしゃ
CLATTER
がっしゃ
I GET IIIT.

KAREN-CHAN!? HOW LONG HAVE YOU BEEN HERE!?

I HAVE BEEN HERE FROM START.
NO WAY!
HOW DID WE MISS EACH OTHER IN THIS TINY SPACE...!?
NOW, NOW, DO NOT SWEAT SMALL STUFF.

HONOKA, YOU ARE SUCH GOOD GIRL TO HELP OUT ON YOUR DAY OFF!
OH, NO!
I'M ONLY HELPING UNTIL NOON TODAY. IT'S NOTHING SPECIAL!
OH, THAT RIGHT.

WE ALL GOING SHOPPING AFTER THIS.
HONOKA, YOU SHOULD COME TOO.
N-NO... I ALREADY HAVE AFTERNOON PLANS WITH KANA-CHAN, AND...
...MOST OF ALL, I HAVEN'T PREPARED MY HEART FOR IT! I COULDN'T!!
PREPARE YOUR HEART?

THANKS FOR INVITING ME.
I'LL SEE YOU AT SCHOOL TOMORROW!

OH!

KANA-CHAN! TOOK YOU LONG ENOUGH!
YOU LOOK LIKE YOU'RE IN AN AWESOME MOOD. WEREN'T YOU WORKING THIS MORNING?
SORRY!

AND AFTER YOU WERE SAYING IT'S A PAIN!
SHHHH!
I DIDN'T SAY THAT!

I WAS JUST THINKING...
...THERE'S HAPPINESS TO BE FOUND ON DAYS WHEN NOTHING HAPPENS TOO. ♡
OH, I BET SOMETHING HAPPENED.
SOMETHING TO DO WITH BLOND HAIR?
Restaurant Matsubara

HER NAME IS AYA KOMICHI.

A HIGH SCHOOL SECOND-YEAR WHO OUT-BLOOMS EVEN THE FLOWERS.

HEY!
ALICE, TRY THIS ON.
OVER YOUR UNIFORM.
SURE THING!

MATCHING OUTFITS... THAT'S SO AWESOME ...
UH... SURE ...

TA-DAAAAAA
MATCHING OUTFITS WITH ALICE...!?

WHAT GOING ON, AYAYA? WHY NOT MATCHING OUTFIT WITH YOUKO!?
かあーっ
BLUSH
B-BUT WE WOULD NEVER SEEM LIKE SISTERS!!

SIS-TERS?
THIS NOVEL'S THEME IS SISTERLY LOVE.
THE LITTLE SISTER IS SO CUTE, AND THEY'RE SO CLOSE THAT THEY EVEN GO OUT IN MATCHING OUTFITS.

SIS-TERS IN MATCH-ING OUT-FITS...?
THERE'S NO WAY I'M DOING THAT. TOO EMBARRASSING.
AND ONEE-CHAN'S CLOTHES AREN'T MY STYLE...

AYAYA... LITTLE SISTER IN NOVEL IS 2-D LITTLE SISTER.
?
HUH?

WHEN I READ BOOKS LIKE THIS, I CAN'T HELP BUT THINK THAT SISTERS ARE GREAT...
COME TO THINK OF IT...
...KAREN SAID THE SAME THING BEFORE, DIDN'T SHE?
THAT SHE WISHED SHE HAD SIBLINGS.

YES, HAVING A LITTLE SISTER IS WONDER-FUL.
ちら…っ
GLANCE
SHINO? WHY ARE YOU LOOKING AT ME?

I'D BE GLAD TO HAVE AYA AS MY BIG SISTER.
ME!?
I ALSO WANT BIG SIS LIKE AYAYA!
GEEZ, KAREN!

AYA-CHAN OUGHT TO MAKE HER HAIR BLOND TOO, TO MAKE THEM LOOK MORE LIKE SISTERS, RIGHT!?
はふぅ
PANT
はふぅ
PANT
MATCH THEM TO THE BIG SISTER!

OKAY, WE DO THIS.
TODAY, WE ARE AYAYA'S LITTLE SISTERS!

WHAT DO YOU MEAN?
WE PLAY SISTERS!
THAT WAY, WE HAVE AYAYA EXPERIENCE WHAT IT LIKE TO LIVE WITH LITTLE SISTER AT HOME.
THERE'S NO SCHOOL TOMORROW ANYWAY.

IF YOU WANT TO STAY OVER, I HAVE TO GET THE OKAY FROM MY MOM.
HOLD ON JUST A MINUTE!
AYA-CHAN SEEMS EXCITED, DOESN'T SHE?

YOU GONNA BE OKAY, THOUGH?
'COS THIS MEANS ALICE WON'T BE HOME FOR THE NIGHT.
はっ
GASP
I FOR-GOT!!

SHINO, DO YOU WANT TO BE AYA'S LITTLE SISTER TOO?
NO! IF I WENT...
...I'D DESTROY THE GOLDEN RATIO OF TWO BLOND LITTLE SISTERS.

HEY, THEN YOU SHOULD COME TO MY PLACE, SHINO!
MAY I?

YEAH, ONE MORE LITTLE SIS IS NO BIG DEAL.
BIG SIS TYPE
IT MUST BE A LOT OF WORK TO BE A BIG SISTER EVERY DAY, YOUKO-CHAN.

ALL RIGHT. TODAY, I'LL BE YOUR BIG SIS.
YOU!?

AYA'S HOUSE
I'M HOME!
WELCOME HOME, DEAR!

COME ON IN.
THANKS FOR HAVING U—
ALICE, THAT NOT RIGHT!

TODAY, WE ARE AYAYA'S BABY SISTERS!
AH!
I GET IT!

I'M HOME, ONEE-CHAN!
H-HEY, ALICE!
HOW WAS KINDER-GARTEN TODAY?
EH!?
ARE WE GOING WITH THAT BIG OF AN AGE GAP!?
......?

HI, GIRLS.
THANK YOU FOR LOOKING AFTER US.
AYA'S MOM

NO YOUKO-CHAN TODAY?
ARRRGH!
WHY ARE YOU BRINGING UP YOUKO!?
SHE IS TSUNDERE WITH EVEN MAMA!

AS OF TODAY, I WILL BE AYAYA'S LITTLE SIS...
NICE TO MEET YOU.
SQUISH
EH...?

ERM...
NO THANK YOU. I DON'T NEED ANOTHER RIGHT NOW?
MOM, IT'S NOT LIKE THAT!!

KAREN! THIS IS SOMEONE ELSE'S HOUSE. DON'T BE A NUISANCE!
OKAY. I WILL BE GOOD.

WE HAVE CAKE.
KACHAK
BUT WE HAD A MISCOMMUNICATION, SO THERE'S ONLY TWO PIECES.

I DON'T NEED ANY. YOU TWO CAN HAVE IT.
I'D FEEL BAD. WE'LL CUT THEM BOTH IN HALF...

...AND WE ROCK-PAPER-SCISSOR FOR LEFTOVER HALF!
GEEZ!
LET ONEE-CHAN HAVE IT!
AH.
THEY SURE COME ACROSS LIKE SISTERS...

YOUKO'S HOUSE
HUUUUH?
IT'S SHINOBU-ONEECHAN.

I CAME OVER!
IT'S JUST YOU?
THAT'S WEIRD.
YEAH, LONG STORY.

KOUTA, MITSUKI...
PLEASE CALL ME "ONEE-CHAN" TODAY...
HUH?
IS THIS A GAME?

YOUKO, YOU SILLY GIRL. LINE YOUR SHOES UP PROPERLY, DEAR.
COME NOW!
WAAAH!
HER PERSONA CHANGED!

ONEE-CHAN, WE GET IN BATH TOGETHER!
WHAT!?
THAT'S A BIT MUCH!
YOUKO AND MIKKI SAY THEY TAKE BATHS TOGETHER.

I GUESS THAT MIGHT BE NORMAL FOR CLOSE SISTERS ...?
THEN...
...I'LL GET IN WITH YOU TODAY.
I'M A LITTLE EMBARRASSED, THOUGH.
STARE
ALIIICE. WHAT ABOUT ME?

THIS BATH POWDER GET VERY, VERY BUBBLY!
I WANT TO RINSE YOUR BACK TOO!
WATCH OUT!
AYA! IF YOU GET IN WITH KAREN, IT'LL GET OUT OF CONTROL!
OH NO! BUBBLES!

GIRLS, THERE'S FRUIT FOR DESSERT.
I WILL EAT! ♡
SPIN
SHE CHANGED HER TUNE QUICK!

HAAH...
THAT'S MUCH BETTER ...
STEAM ほこ
STEAM ほこ
CLATTER ガタ
ガターン CRASH
GYAAAAH!!

BAM
WHAT WAS THAT?
KAREN !?
ARE YOU OKAY !?
AH...
AH...

ONEE-CHAN, I SEE A...A...!
WHAP
WHAT DID YOU SEE!?
WAS IT A GHOST ...!?

A BUG...
THAT'S EVEN SCARIER!

BUT I CLEAN! IT'S NOT EVEN SUMMER! WHY!?
IT HAPPENS SOMETIMES.
AYA-MAMA POPPED OUT TO STORE, AND PAPA IS NOT HOME YET!

AYA... CATCH IT...
TREMBLE
TREMBLE
I CAN HANDLE RHINO BEETLE, BUT THIS TOO MUCH.
BOTH OF THEM ARE COUNTING ON ME!

GLINT
TODAY, I'M THE BIG SISTER ...
I HAVE TO PROTECT THEM.

WHY YOU LEAVE ROOM !?

I'M SORRY... I'M A FAILURE OF A BIG SISTER.
AYA... IT'S NOT YOUR FAULT!

YOU WERE GOOD BIG SISTER TODAY!
BUT AYAYA IS SECOND DAUGHTER.

THIS TIME TO ASK FOR HELP OF ELDEST DAUGHTER!!

OH, YOUKO. DO YOU NOT UNDERSTAND ENGLISH, DEAR?
SHOW IT TO ME.
SOMEBODY HELP ME...
ELDEST DAUGHTER

ONEE-CHAN, YOUR PHONE.

HELLO?
Onee-chan, help!
Aya?
BLUSH

Y— YOU DIDN'T HEAR WHAT YOU THINK YOU HEARD!
AH!
THE BUG ESCAPED OUT WINDOW—

WE CAME BECAUSE WE WERE WORRIED...
'COS YOU HUNG UP ON ME.

...AND IT WAS JUST A BUG?
IT WAS AN EMERGENCY!
A FEW HOURS NO SEE! ♥

YOU CAN'T CALL YOURSELF A BIG SIS IF YOU CAN'T HANDLE THAT MUCH!
SNUB
WELL, IT'S NOT LIKE I WANT TO BE YOUR BIG SISTER!

SHOCK
THEY'RE MORE LIKE SISTERS THAN US!

KAREN-CHAN, WANT A PARFAIT?
"OH ..."

HONOKA... I THINK I GETTING TOO OLD FOR SWEETS.
ガシャーンッ
CRASH
EH!?
WHY !?

I AM ALMOST THIRD-YEAR...I GETTING TOO OLD FOR HONOKA TOO.
すぅぅ…
SHMMM
NO... WAIT !!

"STAND BY ME!!"
ガターンッ
CLATTER
ビクッ
JOLT
!?

はぁーーっ
SIIIGH
URGH...
I'M SO EMBARRASSED!

HONOKA NEVER FALL ASLEEP IN CLASS!
WHAT ON EARTH WERE YOU DREAMING ABOUT?

AT THE SAME TIME, I WAS HAVING A DREAM WHERE I WAS IN A POOL OF BLOND HAIR.
EEEP!
IT...
ゾッ
SHUDDER

...WASN'T THAT ENVIOUS A DREAM!
ARE YOU SURE HERS ISN'T A NIGHTMARE!?

ACTUALLY, SOMETHING'S BEEN ON MY MIND LATELY...
...SO I HAVEN'T BEEN GETTING ENOUGH SLEEP.

COUNSELOR AYAYA
IS IT... LOVE...?
EH?
UM, NO. IT'S NOT THAT.

EXCUSE ME.
WHY DO YOU HAVE THAT!?
MM-HM, MM-HM...
STETHOSCOPE

DR. AYAYA
YOUR HEART RATE IS AT THE SPEED OF LOVE.
IF YOU IGNORE IT, IT'LL GET WORSE!!
AYA-CHAN, WHAT'S COME OVER YOU!?
YOU'VE GOT SOMETHING BAD!

I MIGHT BE ABLE TO HELP. YOU CAN TALK TO ME ANYTIME.
THANK YOU, AYA-CHAN.

BUT EVEN YOU CAN DO NOTHING ABOUT THIS.
BESIDES, TO YOU, I'M SURE IT'S JUST AS...

BLOND ... ...HAIR ...

YOU CALLED?
PWOP
EEEEEEK!

IS THIS NOT THE BLOND HAIR YOU WERE LOOKING FOR?
BADUM
BADUM
NO, YOU JUST STARTLED ME WHEN YOU POPPED OUT OF NOWHERE!

KAREN WAS WORRIED ABOUT YOU EARLIER, YOU KNOW!
!
NOW I'VE MADE EVEN KAREN-CHAN WORRY FOR NO REASON...

IF YOU WANT... I'LL LEND YOU A SIDE OF MY BLOND HAIR.
SWISH
EH!?

EEK! AAAH!
IT'S SO SOOTHING!
IT'S JUST SO INCREDIBLY HEALING!!

OH. SO...
...THE UPCOMING CLASS CHANGE WAS BUGGING YOU.

I SEE...
SORRY!
はっ
GASP
I KNOW IT'S NOT ONLY ME. YOU'RE CONCERNED TOO, AREN'T YOU?

YOU AREN'T?
NO, I'M OKAY.
I'M NOT AS ANXIOUS AS LAST YEAR.
I REALIZED SOMETHING. EVEN IF OUR CLASSES ARE APART, OUR HEARTS WILL ALWAYS BE TOGETHER.

※MENTAL IMAGE
ALICE-CHAN...
IN JUST ONE YEAR, SHE REACHED MENTAL MATURITY!?

WHAT HAPPENED!? YOU'RE LIKE A COMPLETELY DIFFERENT PERSON!!
FU FU...
I'M A NEW WOMAN THIS YEAR...
ALICE VERSION 2

BUT... BUT...THIS YEAR, THE CLASS CHANGE IS COMPLETELY DIFFERENT!
YOU KNOW!
WE HAVE THE CLASS TRIP RIGHT AFTER WE BECOME THIRD-YEARS, REMEMBER!?
YUP!
I CAN HARDLY WAIT!

YOU CAN'T BE IN THE SAME GROUP ON THE TRIP IF YOU'RE IN DIFFERENT CLASSES.
YOU WOULDN'T BE ABLE TO MAKE THE SAME MEMORIES TOGETHER ON OUR LAST BIG HIGH SCHOOL EVENT!

WAAH!
I DON'T WANT THAT!
※MENTAL IMAGE 2
THANK GOODNESS! ALICE-CHAN IS BACK TO NORMAL!!
TE EN SY

WHAT SHOULD WE DO !?
THERE'S NOTHING WE CAN DO BUT CROSS OUR FINGERS. THAT'S WHY I'VE BEEN SO ANXIOUS.

NO!
THERE'S STILL TIME UNTIL WE'RE THIRD-YEARS!
THERE HAS TO BE SOMETHING WE CAN DO!

ALICE-CHAN! YOU'RE SO SMALL, YET SO DEPENDABLE.
NO ONE'S CALLED ME DEPENDABLE BEFORE!
BLUSH
WELL, DO YOU HAVE ANY GOOD IDEAS?

WE SHOULD ENTER INTO DIRECT NEGOTIATIONS WITH SENSEI!
YOU LOOK CUTE, BUT THAT STATEMENT ISN'T!

SENSEI'S KIND. IF WE ASK NICELY, SHE SHOULD GRANT OUR WISHES!
SHE EVEN MADE ME SHINO #2!
YOU TALK ABOUT IT LIKE SANTA CLAUS COMING ON CHRISTMAS...

IT'LL BE OKAY! I'LL ASK WITH A SERIOUS FACE!
FIRM
WOW!

LET'S ROLE-PLAY IT!
"SENSEI, YOU'RE LOOKING BEAUTIFUL TODAY AS ALWAYS. YOUR COOKING IS EXCELLENT TOO. YOU'RE PERFECT."
UM, THANK YOU?
I MEAN, IT DOESN'T FEEL BAD TO HEAR THAT... BUT, UM...

"BY THE WAY, PLEASE PUT ME IN THE SAME CLASS AS SHINO."
YOU MIGHT BE KIND OF BAD AT THIS !!

YOU WANT US TO PUT YOU ALL IN THE SAME CLASS?
YOU'RE CLOSE EVEN WHEN YOU'RE IN SEPARATE CLASSES, AREN'T YOU?

LIKE RIGHT NOW.
YES, BUT IT'S NOT THE SAME!
WE'RE NOT THE ONLY ONES MAKING THE DECISION, SO WE CAN'T PROMISE ANYTHING.

BUT YOU WILL BE JUST FINE.
THE GODS ARE WATCHING YOUR HARD WORK, AFTER ALL.
I'M SURE GOOD THINGS ARE IN STORE FOR YOU!

HARD WORK ...?
BEFORE YOU WORRY ABOUT THE CLASS CHANGE, AREN'T OOMIYA-SAN AND KUJOU-SAN IN DANGER OF FAILING THE YEAR?
はっ
GASP

YO, PEEPS!
HEY, IS ALICE HERE?
2-A
YOUKO-CHAN!

I THINK SHE'S BEEN WITH HONOKA-CHAN SINCE THIS MORNING.
SINCE WHEN WERE THOSE TWO SO CLOSE ...?

ALICE HASN'T SPOKEN TO ME AT SCHOOL AT ALL TODAY. I'M A BIT LONELY.
SOUNDS LIKE ALICE HAS BECOME TOTALLY INDEPENDENT FROM YOU!

※ SHE HAS NOT.
I WANT TO BE IN SHINO'S CLASS!
WHAT SHOULD I DO TO END UP IN KAREN-CHAN'S CLASS?

THIS IS THE LAST RESORT! WE CAN ONLY ASK THE GODS!
WHAAAT!?
THIS GOT FISHY IN AN INSTANT!

HOW DO WE ASK THE GODS?
ALICE-CHAN, I THOUGHT YOU WERE CHRISTIAN?
WHEN IN ROME, DO AS THE ROMANS DO!
WE COULD VISIT A SHRINE A HUNDRED TIMES...

OH, I KNOW!
THAT WOULD BE TOUGH. YOUR KOKESHI DOLL SEEMS LIKE IT WOULD BRING GOOD FORTUNE.
LET'S PRAY TO IT!

GREAT KOKESHI-SAMA!
BOW
BOW
SHINO!
STARE

ACK!
KAREN-CHAN!!
GULP
HONOKA... YOU OKAY?

I SEE. YOU LOSE SLEEP OVER CLASS CHANGE.
OHH...
YEAH...
YOU DON'T GET HUNG UP ON THINGS LIKE THIS, DO YOU, KAREN?

HONOKA! THEY SAY, WHAT HAPPENS TWICE WILL HAPPEN THRICE!
EVEN IF WE SPLIT UP, WE WILL BE THE SAME WHEN WE GO OUT FOR FUN!

SO "NO PROBLEM"!
SHIIINE
THAT'S SUPER OPTIMISTIC!

I BET SHINO WILL SAY SAME THING TOO!
......

N-NOW I FEEL SILLY FOR WORRYING OVER A LITTLE THING LIKE THAT.
I SHOULD TAKE A PAGE OUT OF YOUR BOOK AND THINK POSITIVE, KAREN...
"HA HA!"

BUT I STILL WANT TREATS, EVEN WHEN WE THIRD-YEARS!
DON'T BE OBNOXIOUS!
!

OF—
OF COURSE !!
DON'T SPOIL HER!

THE NEXT DAY
HONOKA, THIS IS FOR YOU.
WHAT? AN ERASER?

THERE'S THIS CHARM. IF YOU WRITE THE NAME OF YOUR CRUSH ON A BRAND-NEW ERASER AND USE UP THE WHOLE THING...
...YOUR LOVE WILL COME TO BE.
FORTUNE-TELLER AYAYA
...... OH, I DIDN'T KNOW.

GOOD LUCK!
THANKS...
AYA-CHAN... I THINK SHE'S FORGOTTEN ABOUT THE CLASS CHANGE, SO...
...I WON'T BRING IT UP FOR NOW.

LOVE EVANGELIST AYAYA

IT IS FIRST DAY OF SPRING BREAK.
キョロ
GLANCE
キョロ
GLANCE
モジ
FIDGET
モジ
FIDGET

HUH?
IT'S KAREN.
ドキーン
THUMP
COTSWOLDS!!

MY HEART BEATING SO FAST.
FOOO!

WHAT IS UP WITH THAT SHOUT?
YOU SURPRISE ME SO MUCH, I SHOUT NAME OF MY HOME-TOWN.
TEE HEE!

YOU SHOPPIN' TOO, KAREN!? AWESOME. WE SHOULD HANG—
BUMP
WE'RE GOING SHOPPING FOR REFERENCE BOOKS.
WANT TO HAVE A STUDY PARTY WITH US, KAREN?

"OH!"
"SORRY." I ALREADY HAVE PLAN WITH SOMEONE ELSE TODAY.
YOU DO?

IT IS OUR FIRST DATE...
BLUSH
...SO I RATHER IT BE JUST THE TWO OF US.

DATE!?

SO...
WHY ARE WE HIDING?
HUM
HUM
I-I JUST HAVE TO KNOW!

ISN'T PEEPING WRONG?
URGH!
SHE'S BEING SECRETIVE! ONCE WE SEE WHO IT IS, WE'LL LEAVE...

KAREN.
!
THEY'RE HERE!!

I HOPE YOU DIDN'T WAIT LONG.
!!?

WHAT'S GOING ON!? IT'S A WOMAN!
A DATE WITH AN OLDER GIRL!?
YUP.

BUT CHECK OUT KAREN'S EYES!
A LOOK OF LOVE!
D'YOU THINK SO?

LOOKS LIKE THE SAME EYES SHE MAKES AT SHINO TO ME...
ズルゥ
SLIP

AHH!
IT SLIPPED OFF AGAIN!
SHINO, YOU CAN LEAVE THAT OFF.

IT'S JUST SHINO!
IT IS FIRST TIME WE HAVE GONE OUT ALONE.
I COULD NOT SLEEP LAST NIGHT!
I WAS TOO EXCITED!
IT IS, NOW THAT YOU MENTION IT.

FINALLY... WE ARE ALONE.
YES, INDEED.
U FU FU!

ごろ
ROLL
ごろ
ROLL
IF AYAYA HEAR THAT SENTENCE ...
...SHE WOULD BE "ROLLING" ALL AROUND RIGHT NOW!
OH MY...
"ROLLING"...

かあーっ
BLUSH
エー
I WOULD NOT!
AYA, HOLD IT IN!
THEY'LL HEAR YOU!

ANYWAY...
THANKS AGAIN FOR TODAY, KAREN.
YEAH.
I WONDER WHERE ALICE IS...?
THESE TWO HANGIN' OUT ALONE IS NEW, THOUGH.

I'M JUST NOT CONFIDENT I CAN PICK OUT A GOOD BIRTHDAY GIFT FOR ALICE ON MY OWN.
I KNOW EVERYTHING ABOUT ALICE. LEAVE IT TO ME!

IT'S ALMOST ALICE'S BIRTHDAY.
OH, DUH!
IN APRIL.
THAT'S WHY SHE WAS BEING SECRETIVE.
SO ALICE WON'T FIND OUT.

LET'S BUY SOME TOO!
BIRTHDAY GIFTS!
GREAT IDEA. WE'LL DO THAT AFTER WE BUY THOSE REFERENCE BOOKS!
FRIENDSHIP BEFORE STUDYING!!
SHE WON'T BUDGE!
AND AFTER THAT, WE'LL HAVE A STUDY PARTY.

BY THE WAY...
...WHAT DID YOU GIVE HER ON LAST BIRTHDAY?
UM, ACTUALLY...

LAST YEAR
"HAPPY BIRTHDAY," ALICE! ♡
AW, YOU SHOULDN'T HAVE!

IT'S A GUIDEBOOK TO ENGLAND!
IT LISTS OUT-OF-THE-WAY SPOTS ONLY THE LOCALS KNOW!
A LOCAL

I'M SO HAPPY...
THANKS...
BUT HER EYES WERE CLEARLY NOT SMILING!

I GUESS THE GIFTS I CHOOSE AREN'T TO ALICE'S TASTES.
I REALIZED THIS RECENTLY.
LIKE THE ROCK FROM ENGLAND...
ONLY RECENTLY?

SHIIINE
BUT YOU'RE GOOD AT SURPRISES, KAREN.
I THOUGHT YOU'D KNOW JUST WHAT ALICE WOULD LIKE!

"DILEMMA!"
I CANNOT SAY "NO" TO YOU, SHINO!
AHH, BUT...
...SINCE IT IS JUST TWO OF US, I WANT TO PLAY LOTS AND LOTS...!

GIVE HER "SHINO COLLECTION."
IT HAS PHOTOS OF SHINO FROM ALL ANGLES!
THIS IS IT.
WHEN DID YOU TAKE THOSE!?
I BORROW IT FROM ISAMI.

OH.
I NEVER GOT THAT PHOTO ALBUM BACK FROM KAREN-CHAN.

ISAMI! WANT SOME SAKURA MOCHI?
I'M MAKING IT NOW.
WHERE'S SHINOBU?
I HAD HER GO OUT TO BUY THE LEAVES.
THIS

SHE'S TAKING A WHILE, ISN'T SHE?
I'M WORRIED!
MAYBE SHE MADE A PIT STOP?
STARE

WAAH!
WHAT!?
SQUEEZE
THERE'S NO ONE TO INTERRUPT, SO I CAN HAVE YOU ALL TO MYSELF.

LOOK, KAREN!
THIS DOLL LOOKS JUST LIKE ALICE. SHE'S SO CUTE! ♡

THAT IS WHAT YOU LIKE, SHINO!
ALICE LIKES MORE JAPANESE-STYLE.
AWW...
BUT...

YES, JAPANESE-STYLE... ESPECIALLY THINGS THAT LOOK LIKE SHINO.
DOES THIS DOLL?
IT NOT LOOK LIKE YOU AT ALL.
SO BLUNT!?

IF YOU WANT SAME TYPE OF DOLL, THIS ONE LOOK LIKE YOU!
EEEK! JAPANESE DOLL
IT'S MORE INTENSE THAN THE KOKESHI. SCARY!

I'D LIKE TO GIVE HER A PRESENT THAT SHE AND I BOTH THINK IS CUTE.
THAT IS VALID POINT.

OKAY...
HOW ABOUT YOU CUSTOMIZE IT? LIKE CHANGE ITS OUTFIT?
I LIKE THAT IDEA! IT'S VERY ORIGINAL...!

THE OUTFIT SHOULD BE MORE FRILLY AND CUTE!
THE HAIR CAN'T BE BLACK EITHER!

IT'S DONE!!
IT LOOK JUST LIKE YOU WEARING BLOND WIG!

NOW ALICE IS SURE TO LOVE THIS TOO!
ALTHOUGH THE FACE IS STILL SCARY...
I-I NOT SURE ...

I CAN SEE ALICE'S REAC-TION NOW...
THANKS...
NO! IT STILL NEED ONE MORE THING!

I KNOW... VOICE! WE PUT SHINO'S VOICE INSIDE, SO SHE CAN FEEL SHINO THERE ANYTIME SHE WANT!
ALICE. ♡

TALKING SHINO DOLL... I WANT ONE TOO!
I CALL PAPA AND HAVE HIM MASS PRODUCE IT!
PLEASE DON'T!

IT GOT QUITE LATE WHILE I HUNG OUT WITH KAREN AFTER THAT...
ARCADE!
KARAOKE!
SHOPPING!
WHEW.
ガチャ CLICK
IS ALICE UPSET...?

SHINO! WHERE HAVE YOU BEEN? I WAS SO WORRIED ABOUT YOU!
WAH!
I'M SORRY. BUT I'M BACK NOW!

WHERE ARE THOSE SAKURA LEAVES?
AH!
I FORGOT ABOUT THEM!
HUH?

DID I JUST SMELL... KAREN ...?
SNIFF くん
SNIFF くん
SO SHARP!?
IT'S—
IT'S YOUR IMAGI-NATION!!

GIRLS! DINNER'S READY!
I'M GOING TO PUT AWAY MY BAG AND CHANGE!
I—

HOW DID SHE CATCH ON SO QUICKLY?
THERE'S STILL SOME TIME UNTIL ALICE'S BIRTH-DAY.
I NEED TO HIDE THE GIFT SOME-WHERE SHE WON'T FIND IT!
PLOP

AH!
FLOP
!?

A... LICE...
SHIVER
GRK

GIRLS! YOU'LL BOTHER THE NEIGH-BORS!

WHAT'S WITH THAT CURSED DOLL...!?
SHAKE
SHAKE
OHH...

IT WAS SUPPOSED TO BE A SURPRISE!
NOW IT'S RUINED!
OH, WE WERE PLENTY SUR-PRISED!

AH.
SHE FIND OUT? WELL, THAT IS GOOD.
HAHAHA!
GOT TOO HYPER, WASN'T THINKING CLEARLY
BACK TO THE DRAWING BOARD
Eh?

POP-POP
APRIL 5TH IS ALICE'S BIRTHDAY!

HAPPY BIRTHDAY, ALICE! ♡
THANKS, YOU GUYS!
YAAAY!
WE GOT YOU A CAKE TOO.
CLAP CLAP

IT'S MISSING A "ONE."
I'M EIGHTEEN!
EH?

OH MY GOSH!
OKAY, BLOW OUT THE CANDLES!
AH!
ALICE-CHAN HAPPY 8TH BIRTHDAY

IT LOOKS RIGHT TO ME?
YEAH.
YEAH, NOTHING'S WRONG HERE.
HUH...!? HOW OLD AM I AGAIN!?

WE'RE KIDDING! IT'S JUST A JOKE!
ONE... TWO... THREE...
I'M SORRY! YOU'RE SO CUTE THAT WE HAD TO TEASE YOU...!

SO LIKE, I'VE GIVEN B-DAY GIFTS, BUT I'VE NEVER DONE A B-DAY PARTY BEFORE.
HAPPY BIRTHDAY
YEAH. IT'LL LAND ON A WEEKDAY, OR YOU JUST CELEBRATE AT HOME.

YOUKO-CHAN, YOU AREN'T VERY GOOD AT REMEMBERING BIRTHDAYS.
URK!
SORRY.
BIRTHDAY PARTIES IN ENGLAND ARE BIGGER BASH!

PAPA HAS GONE BUNGEE JUMPING ON HIS BIRTHDAY!
"BIRTHDAY BUNGEE!"
ENGLAND IS ON AN ENTIRELY DIFFERENT SCALE!
I'M PRETTY SURE THE KUJOU FAMILY IS AN EXCEPTION.

OKAY, YEAH, I USED TO FORGET...
...BUT THIS YEAR, I TOTALLY BOUGHT A B-DAY GIFT FOR ALICE!

SHE WAS REALLY AGONIZING OVER IT.
CHOOSING YOUR GIFT.
REALLY?
AWW!
WELL, YEAH, 'COS I WANT YOU TO LIKE IT!

VOILA! IT'S A NATTO-FLAVORED YUMSTICK!!
I HAD TO TASTE-TEST ALL THE FLAVORS TO PICK IT.
NO! YOUKO!

I TOLD YOU TO GIFT-WRAP IT!!
YOU CAN'T JUST HAND IT TO HER!!
AYA!? THAT'S NOT THE PROBLEM!

NO WORRIES! MY GIFT IS THE GIFT OF A JOKE.
BUT AYA'S GOT AN AWESOME GIFT FOR YA!

WOW, YOUKO! WAY TO PUT THE PRES-SURE ON!
ARGH!
DOESN'T KNOW WHAT AYA'S GIFT IS
WHAT COULD IT BE? I'M SO EXCITED!
WAAAH!

I CAN'T GIVE IT TO YOU HERE. LET'S GO OUTSIDE FOR IT LATER.
HUH?
IS IT THAT BIG!?

YEAH. PLUS, IT'D BE A CRIME TO WALK OFF WITH IT.
ARE YOU SURE I SHOULDN'T WORRY!?

HONOKA AND I CHOOSE GIFT TOGE-THER!
UM, IT'S CLOTHES. I HOPE YOU'LL LIKE IT...

WAH! IT LOOKS WON-DERFUL ON YOU!
YOU HAVE GOOD TASTE.

WHERE DID YOU BUY THIS? I HOPE IT WASN'T TOO EXPEN-SIVE...
IT FROM CHILDREN SECTION AT DEPARTMENT STORE.
AAH!!

KAREN-CHAN! THAT WAS A SECRET!!
SIZE: 140 CM
IT'S NOT WHAT YOU THINK! WE LOOKED IN LOTS OF PLACES. THAT ONE JUST SUITED YOU THE MOST...!!

AS FOR ME...I RACKED MY BRAINS OVER IT...
...BUT IN THE END, I COULDN'T FIND SOMETHING I KNEW ALICE WOULD LIKE, SO...

HERE.
SHINOBU COUPON
SHINOBU COUPON
SWIP
すっ
SHINOBU COUPONS ...?

USE THESE COUPONS TO ASK ME TO DO ANYTHING YOU WANT!
LIKE GIVE YOU A SHOULDER MASSAGE, OR CLEAN FOR YOU!
OH, IT'S LIKE A MOTHER'S DAY GIFT.
ANY-THING ...!?

I'M SORRY IT'S NOT SOME-THING BETTER.
NO, IT'S OKAY!
IT'S EVEN BETTER THAN A GIFT CERTI-FICATE!
WHAT!?
REALLY!?

I DON'T WANT TO WASTE THESE. I'LL STORE THEM AWAY CARE-FULLY.
NO, PLEASE USE THEM!
IF YOU DON'T USE THEM, THEY'RE JUST ORDINARY PAPER!

BUT...
...I DON'T NEED ANYTHING AS LONG AS I HAVE YOU WITH ME, SHINO!
ALICE!!

ぎゅーっ
SQUEEZE
OKAY!
THEN I WON'T LEAVE YOUR SIDE!! NOT EVEN FOR AN INSTANT!!

CLOSE...
THAT'S TOO CLOSE...

すっ
SWUP
BATH-ROOM...

TEA...
さっ
SWIP
HERE YOU ARE.

ぎゅうぎゅう
SMOOSH
SMOOSH

SHINO... THAT'S PLENTY.
す…っ
SWUSH
A RIFT OPENED BETWEEN THEIR HEARTS!!
MUSTA BEEN TOO SUFFO-CATING.

ANYWAY... IF ALICE'S BIRTHDAY IS HERE...
...THAT MEANS WE'RE ALREADY THIRD-YEARS.

HEH...
AYA-CHAN?

IT'S SPRING, HUH?
SPRING... THE SEASON OF PARTING...

FU FU...
SOME-THING'S WRONG WITH AYA-CHAN!!
SHE LOOK LIKE SHE KNOW SOMETHING!

AYA-CHAN... HAS SHE REALIZED THAT THE CLASS CHANGE IS COMING UP...?
FINALLY...

AYA!
I'M DYING TO KNOW WHAT YOUR GIFT IS!
RIGHT, OF COURSE. READY TO GO?

FIRST, PUT THIS ON!
IT'S DARK!
I WANT THE REVEAL TO BE A SURPRISE.
EYE MASK

IT'S OKAY. YOU CAN TRUST ME!
ゾロゾロ
FILE
FILE
STARE
THE PEOPLE ON THE STREET ARE ALL STARING!

THE PARK
さああー
SWIIISH
YOU CAN TAKE OFF THE EYE MASK NOW.
MY GIFT TO YOU IS THE BEAUTY OF THESE SAKURA TREES.

AREN'T THEY JUST GORGEOUS?
Y... YEAH!

IT'S A ROMANTIC PRESENT, AND VERY AYA...
...BUT I'VE BEEN IN JAPAN FOR TWO YEARS. I'VE SEEN THE SAKURA MANY TIMES. I SAW THEM JUST YESTERDAY!
BUT I AM HAPPY, AND SHE DID DO THIS FOR ME...

DOES THIS COUNT AS A REAL GIFT?
I WANNA HAVE A PICNIC UNDER THESE.
SHINO!?

WELP, SPRING BREAK'S ALMOST OVER.
GASP
MIRACU-LOUSLY, THE TWO OF US PASSED OUR SECOND YEAR. WE'RE IN A "HAPPY" MOOD!

MOVING UP A YEAR... THE CLASS CHANGE ...
SHE'S GOT THAT LOOK AGAIN ...
AYA-CHAN HAS A CASE OF THE NERVES BECAUSE SHE DOESN'T LIKE CLASS CHANGES!

HONOKA.
I'M NOT BOTHERED BY THAT.
IT'S NOT LIKE IT WAS AT THE START OF THE SECOND YEAR. I'VE GROWN TOO.

EVEN IF I WAS THE ONLY ONE TO END UP WITH NO FRIENDS IN MY CLASS ...
...IT WOULD BE NO BIG DEAL!
TREMBLE プル
TREMBLE プル
DON'T IMAGINE THE VERY WORST POSSI-BILITY!

IF WE END UP IN DIFFER-ENT CLASSES, DON'T FORGET ME, OKAY ...?
SNAP OUT OF IT!
GEEZ!
MENTAL MATURITY AND PUTTING ON A STRONG FRONT AREN'T THE SAME THING !!

AYA, YOU SAY YOU'D BE OKAY APART FROM THE REST OF US.
BUT I WANT US TO BE TOGE-THER!

IF I GOT SEPA-RATED FROM YOU AGAIN, AYA, I'D MISS YA TOO MUCH.

ALL OF US SHOULD BE TOGE-THER!
WAAAH!
YOUKO-CHAN'S CRYING!!

I...
じ
わっ
TEARY
I...

I...
...WANT THAT EVEN MORE!

NO, I DO MORE!
ME TOO!
I DO TOO!
DON'T TURN IT INTO A COMPE-TITION!

AYA, I'LL GIVE YOU ONE OF MY SHI-NOBU COU-PONS.
SHINO CAN DO SOME-THING ABOUT THIS, I KNOW IT!
EH!?
SHINO! MAKE US BE IN THE SAME CLASS ...!

OKAY! PLEASE PUT YOUR MIND AT EASE!
IF WE CAN'T BE IN THE SAME CLASS...
...I'LL REPEAT THE YEAR!
THAT'S POINT-LESS, SHINO!

THEN I'LL GO BLOND!
THAT MEAN EVEN LESS!
THE NEW SCHOOL YEAR
WHAT DID I TELL YOU? SHINO IS AMAZ-ING!
I AGREE.
OH, BUT IT WASN'T ME...

YOU GUYS...
HERE'S TO ANOTHER FUN SCHOOL YEAR TOGETHER!

WHERE'S KAREN?
SHE'S IN THE CLASS NEXT DOOR.
WELL...
WITH HER, IT FEELS LIKE SHE'S IN OUR CLASS NO MATTER WHERE SHE IS.
LET'S ALL GO OUT FOR FUN!

TOGETHER FOR ALL THREE YEARS OF HIGH SCHOOL ...
IT'S NOTHING SHORT OF A MIRACLE. RIGHT...

...KAREN-CHAN!?
YES!
IT IS SAME CLASS SPLIT AS FIRST YEAR.

BUT SOMETHING ABOUT YOU IS DIFFERENT FROM HONOKA BACK THEN.
"YAY!"
WHAT DOES THAT MEAN!? KAREN-CHAN!?

WE'RE THIRD-YEARS!

THE KIND OF PERSON WHO CAN'T SLEEP BEFORE BIG DAYS
WELL, I'M ALREADY UP, AND IT IS THE START OF A NEW SCHOOL YEAR.
そわ
FIDGET
そわ
FIDGET
I'M AFRAID I'LL OVER-SLEEP IF I GO BACK TO BED, SO I'LL JUST STAY UP...

I WOKE UP TOO EARLY!!
TWO HOURS BEFORE HER ALARM

IT'S SO RARE FOR YOU TO OVER-SLEEP!
I GOT CARRIED AWAY! I'M SO SORRY!

SHE ENDED UP FALLING BACK ASLEEP.

YOU'RE 3-B'S HOMEROOM TEACHER THIS YEAR, RIGHT, KARASUMA-SENSEI?
YES, I AM.
AND YOU'RE IN CHARGE OF CLASS A!

KUJOU-SAN...IS IN YOUR CLASS, YES?
IN CLASS B.
SHE IS!
IT'S THE FIRST TIME I'VE BEEN HER HOMEROOM TEACHER!

MEMORIES WITH KUJOU-SAN
KUZEHASHI-SENSEI!
HA HA HA
HAPPIS MAKE ME HAPPY!
CLENCH
SHE CAN BE A BAD STUDENT, BUT SHE'S A GOOD AND SWEET GIRL AT HEART.
I APPRECIATE YOU GIVING HER YOUR GUIDANCE!
SENSEI ...
ARE YOU HER MOTHER?

YOU WERE ALWAYS WORRYING ABOUT KAREN-SAN.
GIGGLE
NOT JUST KUJOU-SAN... THEY ARE ALL THIRD-YEARS NOW, SO...

I KNOW JUST WHAT YOU MEAN.
WE'VE WATCHED THEM SINCE THEY WERE LITTLE FIRST-YEARS.
THINKING OF THEM GRADUATING BRINGS TEARS TO MY EYES.

SENSEI!? YOU'RE ALREADY CRYING!
ERK
BLOOSH
BUT WE TEACHERS CAN'T BE CRYING!

SO I'VE BEEN WATCHING DOCUMENTARIES OF CHICKS LEAVING THE NEST LATELY, TO MENTALLY TRAIN MYSELF.
WON'T THAT MAKE IT WORSE!?
HIC!
HIC!

WE NEED TO FOCUS ON THE NEW TERM FIRST!
RIGHT, THE SCHOOL YEAR'S ONLY JUST BEGUN!
RIGHT... I HAVE A NEW CLASS.
STARTING OFF ON THE RIGHT FOOT IS IMPORTANT.
GLINT
I'LL NEED TO GIVE THEM GENTLE GUIDANCE TOO...
...BUT SOMETIMES, AN EDUCATOR MUST HARDEN HER HEART AND BE SEVERE—

BUMP
AH!
!
LOOK WHERE YOU'RE WALKING—

I'M SORRY...
TWINGE

FRET
FRET
AH... AH...
CAR-TELET-SAN...
KUZE-HASHI-SENSEI!

I'M GLAD YOU'RE MY HOME-ROOM TEACHER THIS YEAR.
THANK YOU IN ADVANCE.
BOW
SWOON
TH-THE PLEASURE IS ALL MINE...

THAT IS 180° FROM HOW YOU HANDLE ME...
STARE
AH!
KUJOU-SAN!?

KUZE-HASHI-SENSEI, I DID NOT KNOW YOU LIKED TINY GIRLS!!
BAH!
D—
DON'T BE ABSURD!
KAREN! WHAT DO YOU MEAN, TINY!?

BUT YOU BROKE INTO SMILE.
ALICE!
STIFFEN
I DID NO SUCH THING! SEE? I'M THE SAME AS USUAL.

...CAN I HELP YOU?
YOU'RE STARING...
NO...
I JUST THINKING, I WISH YOU WERE MY HOMEROOM TEACHER THIS YEAR TOO...

...!
KUJOU-SAN!!
FLIP
AH!
KARA-SUMA-SENSEI! I SO "HAPPY" YOU ARE MY HOMEROOM TEACHER!!

WHY ...?
SENSEI, PLEASE BE EXTRA STRICT WITH THIS ONE!
OKAY!

CLASS B
LET'S MAKE THIS A GREAT YEAR, FOLKS!

WHISPER
KANA-CHAN, I'M SO GLAD WE GOT TO BE TOGETHER FOR ALL THREE YEARS TOO.
WE ARE CLASS BUDDIES!
WHISPER
GLAD TO BE!
AH!
TALK-ING IN CLASS!

BE EXTRA STRICT!
BAD!
HEY! PAY ATTENTION !!
AH!

むぎゅーっ
SQUOOSH
YOUR PUNISH-MENT IS A HUG!
SHE'S SUPER-SOFT.

CLASS A
I'M LOOKING FORWARD TO HAVING KUZEHASHI-SENSEI!
YEAH! I ONLY KNOW HOW SHE IS IN HOME EC.

LAST YEAR, KAREN ALWAYS SAID SHE WAS STRICT...
SHE DID.
I THINK SHE'S NICER THAN SHE WAS AT FIRST.
I BET SHE'LL GREET US WITH A SMILE...

I'M YOUR HOMEROOM TEACHER.
CRACKLE
AKARI KUZEHASHI!

H... HUH?
SHE REVERTED?

IT FEELS LIKE SHE'D GET VERY ANGRY IF YOU SLEPT IN CLASS...
ROAR
ゴオオオ
EVEN KARASUMA-SENSEI GETS MAD ABOUT THAT.
I FEEL A TERRIFYING PRESSURE COMING OFF HER.

WELL...
...SHE IS IN CHARGE OF STUDENTS WHO GOTTA PREPARE FOR COLLEGE EXAMS.
!
SO SHE'S MAKING A POINT OF BEING STRICT FOR OUR BENEFIT!
THAT IS SO KIND OF HER!

THIS CLASS IS DANGEROUS.
SMALL ANIMAL AURA
I CAN FEEL MY FACE SOFTENING, ESPECIALLY WHEN I SEE CARTELET-SAN.

TO MAINTAIN MY DIGNITY AS AN EDUCATOR...
...I HAVE TO WITHSTAND IT...!
プル
TREMBLE
プル
TREMBLE
?
IS IT JUST ME OR ARE THE CORNERS OF HER MOUTH TREMBLING?

OKAY, KIDS! THAT CONCLUDES MORNING HOMEROOM.
STAAAND!
BOWWW!

THEY'RE ALL GOOD KIDS. SENSEI'S PLEASED.
HAAAH!
OH?

KUZEHASHI-SENSEI, GOOD WORK—
JOLT
ビクッ
SENSEI...
GLOOM

I'M EXHAUSTED...
WHITE AS A GHOST ON DAY ONE...!?

IS YOUR "MY STUDENTS ARE SO CUTE THAT I START GLARING" CONDITION BACK?
NO! I OVERCAME THAT LAST YEAR!

IT'S THE OPPOSITE! THEY'RE SO CUTE THAT I START TO BREAK INTO A SMILE!
OH MY.
I DON'T THINK YOU NEED TO STOP YOURSELF, THOUGH?

BUT I'VE BEEN FEELING THESE TWINGES IN MY HEART ALL DAY.
I FELT IT SEVERAL TIMES.
WHEN I GET HOME, I'LL BE FAWNING OVER MY CAT TOO.

IF THIS GOES ON, I MIGHT DIE OF CUTENESS!
AHHHH!
KUZEHASHI-SENSEI...

SERIOUS

KAREN, HOW'S CLASS A?
KARASUMA-SENSEI IS VEEEERY NICE!
I'M JEALOUS OF YOU, KAREN!

IT FEELS LIKE SHE'D BABY YOU A LOT. I'M WORRIED.
HONOKA'S SOFT ON YOU TOO.
IT OKAY!

AHEM!
I AM A THIRD-YEAR TOO. I DO NOT NEED SCOLDING TO BE GOOD!
WHAT A GOOD GIRL!

HOW MUCH DID SHE INCREASE YOUR ALLOWANCE THIS TIME?
IF YOU'RE GOOD...
...I'LL INCREASE YOUR ALLOWANCE!
GET THIS... BY 500 YEN!

IT'S IMPORTANT TO HAVE GOALS OR RESOLUTIONS.
I'VE RESOLVED TO TRY HARDER THIS SCHOOL YEAR TOO.

TO MAKE MY DREAM COME TRUE TOO!
GASP
SHINO'S STARTED TO FACE REALITY!

I'VE ALREADY STARTED TO BE ABLE TO DO SOMETHING I COULDN'T DO LAST YEAR.
THAT'S GREAT! WHAT IS IT?

HAND STANDS, BUT I CAN'T SHOW YOU RIGHT NOW SINCE I'M WEARING A SKIRT.
NO NEED.
I DON'T CARE ABOUT THAT...

ISN'T THERE ANY-THING ELSE?
THERE IS!
I CAN IMITATE THE CALL OF THE JAPANESE BUSH WARBLER.

HOH...
HOKEKYO.
!?
D-DUUUDE!!

HOW DID YOU DO THAT?
CLAMOR
わい
CLAMOR
わい
THAT'S MY SHINO!
PLEASE TEACH TO ME TOO!!
SIGH

I...
...GOTTA KEEP IT TOGETH-ER.
A RESOLUTION

WE'RE HOME!
WELCOME BACK!

SINCE WE WERE SPLIT UP DURING CLASSES LAST YEAR...
...BEING TOGETHER ALL DAY FEELS FRESH AGAIN!
YOU SAID IT!

IT FEELS LIKE HAVING ROAST BEEF EVERY DAY!

D-DOES THAT MEAN IT'S TOO HEAVY!?
?
NO.
IT MEANS I'M HAPPY.
ARE YOU SURE!?

LUNCH BREAK
IT IS BENTO TIME!
POP
PUH-POP
THE BEST PART OF THE SCHOOL DAY—!
"YEAAAAH!"

LUCKY... I WANNA EAT THAT TOO!
HUH!?
C'MON, IT LOOKS SO GOOD!
SWITCH WITH ME!
!
O-OKAY, I GUESS.

AYA, YOUR LUNCHES ARE ALWAYS SO CUTE.
HOME-MADE
THANKS.
YOUR COOKING SKILL IS IMPROVING BY LEAPS AND BOUNDS!

WHOO-HOO!
WHITE RICE & A SINGLE PLUM
HEY!!

LOOKS LIKE YOUKO'S MUM OVER-SLEPT TODAY...
SORRY. I RAN OUT OF TIME. ♥
LOVE, MOM
ON THE ONE DAY I STOPPED MYSELF FROM WOLFING MY LUNCH DOWN EARLY...
OH MY.
IT'S HARD GETTING UP EARLY EVERY DAY TO MAKE IT.

I CAN'T TAKE THIS! I GOTTA EAT AYA'S HOME-MADE LUNCH!
TASTE OF MOM'S HOME COOKING, "PLEASE"!
"PLEASE!!"
I AM NOT YOUR MOM!!

BUT...
...IF YOU WANT IT THAT BADLY, I SUPPOSE I COULD MAKE ONE FOR YOU...
YOU MEAN IT!?

ON ONE CONDITION.
THUD
!?

I'LL ONLY DO IT IF YOU FINISH ALL OF THESE WORK-BOOKS.
WHAAA—!?
THAT CONDITION IS TOO HARSH!!
YES, YOUKO-CHAN CAN'T DO ALL OF THAT ALONE!
THIS IS TYRANNY!
MOUNTAIN
SHE WON'T HAVE TO.
THIS IS FOR THE THREE OF YOU—SHINO, YOUKO, AND KAREN!

DASH
DON'T RUN AWAY!!

THE NEXT DAY
YOU-KO'S HOUSE
ズゥーン
GLOOM

DOING THE WORK ON YOUR OWN IS WHAT WILL REALLY MAKE IT STICK.
I CAN'T HELP YOU, BUT I WISH YOU LUCK!
WE DON'T EVEN HAVE ALICE, MY LAST RAY OF HOPE?

ALL RIGHT! LET'S SHOW THEM THAT EVEN WE CAN DO IT IF WE PUT OUR MINDS TO IT!
SHINO, YOUR EYES TURN GOLDEN!
THIS ONE IS WORKBOOK.
MATH WORKBOOK
BLOND MAIDENS

EYES: GOLD

WHAT, ARE WE THE THREE STOOGES!?

WAAH!

SHE ADMIT IT HERSELF!

I KNOW JAPANESE PROVERB THAT IS PERFECT FIT FOR THIS SITUATION.
AH!
I KNOW THE ONE YOU MEAN.
IF I REMEMBER RIGHT, IT'S...

..."THREE PEOPLE TOGETHER HAVE MONT SAINT-MICHEL."
THAT NOT HOW IT END.
THEY HAVE "MOTORCYCLE"!
THOSE AREN'T EVEN JAPANESE WORDS.

IT'S OBVIOUSLY SUPPOSED TO BE MONJAYAKI! YOU KNOW, THE FOOD!
YEESH!
STARE

NO...
IT'S "THE WISDOM OF MANJUSHRI, THE BODHISATTVA"...
STAAARE
THIS IS CLOSER TO THE PROVERB "MANY WOMEN, MANY WORDS"...

COME TO THINK OF IT... ...YOU TWO HAVE NEVER BEEN IN THE SAME CLASS, HAVE YOU?
OH YEAH. NO.

IF THE THREE OF US WERE ALL IN THE SAME CLASS...
UHHH... UHHH...
CRUD! I DON'T KNOW THE ANSWER!

SHINO...
SHE'S ASLEEP!
KAREN?
SHE'S ASLEEP TOO!!

UGH...!
SO I CAN ONLY RELY ON MYSELF...
ZZZZ...
YOU'RE ALL GONNA SLEEP!?

AHHH!
IT IS KOUTA AND MIKKI!
OOPS...
HELLO! WE CAME OVER!

PLAY WITH US!
WE'RE BUSY STUDYING. GO PLAY BY YOURSELVES, 'KAY?
AWWW!

PLAY WITH ME! I GIVE YOU CANDY!
KAREN-ONEECHAN, YOU'RE NICER THAN OUR REAL SISTER!
WAAH!

THEY'VE GOTTEN AWFULLY ATTACHED TO KAREN, HMM?
WHEN DID THAT HAPPEN?

YOU TWO BECOME PART OF MY FAMILY.
HUH?
CAN WE?
HOLD IT!!

I'M WAY COOLER THAN KAREN!
LIKE, I'M A HUNDRED TIMES STRONGER!
WATCH THIS!
I CAN SPEAK ENGLISH.

A-AMAZING!!
NATIVE SPEAK-ERS ARE SO DIFFER-ENT!
WE'LL GET THROUGH THE ENGLISH WORK-BOOK EASILY WITH KAREN HERE!

ACK!
IT IS ONLY "JOKE," YOUKO!!
I'M DOWN FOR THE COUNT...
YOU'RE OUR ONE AND ONLY BIG SISTER.

YOUKO-CHAN! PHYSICAL STRENGTH IS MORE IMPORTANT THAN ACADEMIC STRENGTH!
SO PLEASE CHEER UP!
I-IS IT REALLY?

I ALSO SCORE LOW ON TESTS...
...BUT MY LOVE FOR ALICE IS STRONGER THAN ANYONE'S.

IF THERE WAS AN ALICE TEST, I WOULD GET 100%!
WHAT ABOUT ON KAREN TEST?
I'D GET 100%, OF COURSE! WITH A "GOOD WORK" FLOWER DRAWING AND TWO CIRCLES!

WHAT ABOUT ON AN ENGLISH TEST?
I'D GET A BIG, RED "F"!

WE GOT THIS! AS LONG AS WE WORK HARD, EVEN WE CAN MANAGE!
YEAH!
LET'S GIVE IT OUR BEST SHOT! FOR AYA'S LUNCH!

... HUH?
I'M SOLVING IT...I'M SOLVING IT!!
SCRIBBLE
MATH USED TO BE SO DIFFICULT FOR ME, BUT NOW I CAN DO IT WITH MY EYES CLOSED!

THANKS, AYA...YOU WANTED TO SHOW US THAT WE HAD IT IN US IF WE JUST BUCKLED DOWN, RIGHT?
WELL, YOU WOKE ME UP...
......
Zzzzz!

CRAAASH
WAKE UP!
AH!
IT WAS ALL A DREAM !?

YOU'RE ALL HOPE-LESS. WE'LL HELP YOU OUT.
WE CAN'T WATCH THIS TRAVESTY.
WAIT A SEC. GRADE SCHOOL KIDS WON'T KNOW THIS STUFF!

STAAARE
BUT... YOU GUYS HAVEN'T GOTTEN ANYWHERE.
AT THE RATE YOU'RE GOING, YOU'LL SPEND THE REST OF YOUR LIVES ON IT AND STILL NEVER FINISH ...

IT'S ABSO-LUTELY TRUE!
I HAVE NO WORDS!!
DO YOU TWO HAVE NO PRIDE !?

MEAN-WHILE
SIZZLE

ALL DONE WITH THE ROLLED OME-LETTES?
YUP, IT'S ALL DONE!
WOW!
GREAT JOB!
EH HEH HEH!

OKAY, OUR SPECIALLY MADE LUNCH IS COMPLETE!
BUH-BAM
WAAAH! IT'S LIKE A SPECIAL NEW YEAR'S FOOD BOX!!

ACT NOW, AND WE'LL THROW IN ONE MORE FOR FREE!!
BUH-BUH-BAM
YOU MADE TOO MUCH!!

WE CAN'T FINISH ALL OF THIS.
YOUKO HAS A BIG APPETITE. IT'LL BE FINE!
OOPS. I GOT TOO INTO IT.

I HOPE THEY'LL LIKE IT ...
THEY WILL!

THIS IS THE BEST LUNCH I'VE EATEN IN MY LIFE, AYA...

IT'S SO DARN TASTY ...
POSE
WHO ARE YOU!?
I'M DOING A YOUKO IM-PRES-SION...
IT'S SO UNLIKE HER, IT'S SHOCK-ING!!

ピンポーン
DING
DONG
YOUKO SHOULD BE READY TO ASK FOR OUR HELP IN TEARS BY NOW.
INOKUMA
I HOPE SHINO AND KAREN ARE FOCUSING TOO.

HELLO!
ガチャ…
KACHAK
WE'VE BEEN WAITING.
HUH? YOU HAVE?

NO, THAT'S NOT RIGHT!

YOU THREE NEED TO GET A BETTER HANDLE ON THE BASICS!
PICTURE: GETTING TUTORED BY A GRADE SCHOOL KID
YES, MA'AM.
IT'S JUST AS YOU SAY.

IT'S JUST ABOUT NOON.
ちゃらーーん
SPARKLE
ALICE AND I MADE THIS LUNCH. LET'S DIG IN.

HERE'S SOME TEA.
WOW!
ARE YOU THREE GOOD?
WE ARE NOT GOOD! THIS IS A LIVING HELL!

YOU CAN EAT SOME IF YOU FINISH FIVE PAGES EACH.
FIVE PAGES... WE COULD DO THAT!

RAAAAH!
AYA-ONEE-CHAN KNOWS HOW TO MAKE THEM WORK.

OUR CLASS TRIP IS RIGHT AROUND THE CORNER.
AHHHH...
I CAN HARDLY WAIT—!

WHAT'S OUR MONEY LIMIT ON SNACKS?
THIS ISN'T A KIDDIE FIELD TRIP.
PRIORITIES! THERE ARE THINGS YOU NEED BEFORE FOOD!
THAT'S RIGHT! DO THE BOTH OF YOU HAVE YOUR PASSPORTS?

PASS-PORTS?
YOU DON'T KNOW ABOUT THEM?
NO...
THEY'RE ABOUT THIS BIG, AND...
WE KNOW THAT...

IN THIS SHAPE ...
TAK
TAK
YOU DON'T NEED TO DRAW IT ON THE BLACK-BOARD!!
DAY DUTY

HUH !?
ARE WE NOT GOING TO ENGLAND FOR THE CLASS TRIP!?
WHERE'D YOU GET THAT IDEA!?
THE DESTINATIONS ARE NARA AND KYOTO.
THE TYPICAL.

THUD
NO...
BUT I EVEN MASTERED ENGLISH JUST FOR THIS...
WHAT ...!?

YOU MASTERED...
...ENGLISH ...?

I'M SORRY! I EXAG-GERATED A LITTLE !!
YEAH, WE KNOW !!

OH, SHINO ...
KYOTO DIALECT IS WHAT YOU NEED TO MASTER!
KYOTO PHRASEBOOK

COME ON IN, Y'ALL!
Y'ALL MUST BE PLUMB TUCKERED OUT!
MUCH OBLIGED!
DON'CHA DARE!
WHOOOOA!

I-IT'S PERFECT KYOTO DIALECT !!
AH... AHHH ...

I'LL STUDY UP!
THAT IS SO ALICE, Y'HEAR !?
YOU DON'T NEED TO CHANGE YOUR SPEECH TO GO THERE!!
KYOTO

GEEZ, YOU'RE ALREADY PRETTY PUMPED FOR THIS.
IT WOULDN'T BE AN EXAGGERATION TO SAY THAT I CAME TO JAPAN JUST FOR THIS DAY!
HUH!?
DIDN'T YOU COME TO JAPAN TO SEE ME!?

IT IS OUR FIRST OVER-NIGHT TRIP TOGETHER! I AM SO HAPPY!
"YAAAY!"
YEP!
I'M GETTIN' REAL EXCITED NOW TOO!

SO EXCITED! YAAAY!
キャっ
YEEK!
キャっ
YEEK!
THEY ARE SUCH KIDS ...

WHEE!
ぐるぐるぐ
SPIN SPIN SPIN
JOIN US, AYAYA!
WHAT THE HECK!?

CALM DOWN!
THE CLASS TRIP ISN'T ALL FUN AND GAMES.
YOU HAVE TO FOLLOW THE ITINERARY AND THE RULES.
GEEZ, YOU'RE TOO SERIOUS.

KAREN LIKES TRAVEL-ING...
...SO SHE SHOULD KNOW THE DOS AND DON'TS.
GO ON, TELL THEM!

THERE IS SAYING. "WHAT HAPPENS IN KYOTO STAYS IN KYOTO"...

THAT IS ALL.
OHHHH!
THAT WON'T HELP THEM AT ALL!

CLASS A
CHOOSE YOUR GROUPS!

I'M GLAD WE'RE ALL TOGETHER.
IT WILL BE A LITTLE LONELY WITHOUT KAREN, THOUGH.
WE MAY BE IN DIFFERENT CLASSES, BUT WE'LL HAVE PLENTY OF CHANCES TO MEET UP.
YEAH, IT WILL...

YES, THIS IS TRUE. YOU WILL SEE ME!
YUP!
AH-HA-HA-HA!

HAHA—
GO BACK TO YOUR CLASSROOM!

NEXT...
REGARDING ITEMS YOU MAY BRING ON THE CLASS TRIP...

I HAVE A LOT OF STUDENTS WHO SEEM LIKE THEY COULD GET LOST DURING THE TRIP.
FRET
FRET
ハラハラ
SPEAKING OF LOST...
DAAAZE
ぼけーっ

MY CAT GOT OUTSIDE AND ENDED UP LOST RECENTLY.
THANKS TO THE COLLAR, THE WHOLE THING WAS RESOLVED WITHOUT INCIDENT.

SO DON'T FORGET YOUR COLLARS, TO KEEP ANYONE FROM GETTING LOST.
LIKE THIS!
WHAT IN THE —!?

CLASS B
THANKS FOR HAVING ME IN YOUR GROUP!

WOULD YOU RATHER HAVE BEEN IN THE SAME GROUP AS ALICE-CHAN AND FRIENDS?
NO. I AM GLAD I IN YOUR GROUP!

BESIDES, I CAN USE CLONE TECHNIQUE. "NO PROBLEM!"
HEH! HEH! HEH!
A CLONE TECHNIQUE!?

C...
COULD I HAVE ONE OF YOUR CLONES!?
BADUM BADUM
TOO BAD. THEY ARE AFTER-IMAGES.
HEY!
SHUP SHUP SHUP

WHERE YOU WANNA GO DURING OUR FREE TIME?
OH MAN, I'M TOO HYPED!
GOOD GRIEF!
TONE THE EXCITEMENT DOWN. YOU'LL HURT YOURSELF!

SO YOU SAY, BUT YOU'RE GRINNIN' AS YOU READ THAT GUIDEBOOK.
!
I AM NOT GRINNING!
TRIP GUIDEBOOK
ばっ WHAP

YOU DON'T NEED TO HIDE IT!
ARGH, NOT YOU TOO!
TRIP GUIDEBOOK
BLUSH かぁー

I TOLD YOU, I'M NOT GRINNING!
DUMMY!
パァァー SHIINE
YUP! THAT IS A GREAT SMILE!

HAAH...

HAAAH...
SHE REALLY DID CONVINCE HERSELF WE WERE GOING TO ENGLAND...
SIGHTSEEING IN ENGLAND
London

FREEZE
SHINO! I WANT TO BUY PAJAMAS FOR THE CLASS TRIP.
COULD YOU COME SHOP-PING WITH ME THIS WEEK-END?

WHOOSH
I'D LOVE TO!! LET'S BUY MATCH-ING PJS!
FRILLY, GIRLY ONES—
I...
I'M GLAD YOU SEEM BETTER!

THREE NIGHTS AND FOUR DAYS, HUH?
KOUTA AND MIKKI WILL MISS YOU.
CHIPS

SHOCK
...I HEARD THAT CATS FORGET THEIR MASTER IN THREE DAYS...
HEY, CUT IT OUT!
THEY WOULD NEVER FORGET ME...

ONEE-CHAN? WHO'S THAT...?
O-OR WOULD THEY...?
YOUKO !?

HONOKA'S ROOM
KANA-CHAN, I'M GOING TO TAKE A NAP NOW.
SORRY IT'S SUDDEN.
WHAT !?
BUT I JUST CAME OVER!!

PEOPLE MIGHT SEE MY SLEEPING FACE ON THE TRIP, RIGHT?
I'M GOING TO BE SO EMBARRASSED IF I'M SLEEPING WITH MY EYES OPEN!

ONCE I FALL ASLEEP, TAKE A PHOTO OF ME.
THEN I CAN CHECK IT!

ZZZ
SNAP
WHAT AM I EVEN DOING?

BADUM
BADUM
THE CLASS TRIP IS HERE AT LONG LAST...
I NEED TO GET FOCUSED!

THE CLASS TRIP IS GOING TO BE A BLAST!
WHEEE! ♡
I'M GOING TO EAT YUMMY FOODS UNTIL I'M READY TO BURST! ♡

WILL YOU VISIT JISHU SHRINE WITH ME?
THIS IS NOT A PERSONAL VACATION!!

COMMIT THE ENTIRE TRIP ITINERARY TO MEMORY BY TOMORROW!
THERE WILL BE A TEST!
KUZEHASHI-SENSEI, YOU'RE A TRUE TEACHER!

THERE!
I FINISHED THE PLAN. ALL THAT'S LEFT IS TO WAIT FOR THE BIG DAY!
I'M ALL READY TOO!
THIS IS MY NIGHT-CAP FOR THE TRIP!

LUCKY YOU, GOING ON A CLASS TRIP.
IS THIS YOUR PLAN FOR YOUR FREE TIME?
ALICE MADE US A SCHEDULE DOWN TO THE MINUTE.

...UH-OH. YOU DON'T HAVE ENOUGH TIME TO BUY SOUVENIRS.
DON'T?
I THOUGHT I ALLOT-TED PLENTY OF TIME FOR THAT.

BUT THERE ARE SO MANY THINGS I'D LIKE YOU TO BUY ME.
SOUVENIR LIST
SLIDE
THAT'S SO MUCH!
WE'LL USE UP ALL OUR TIME JUST BUYING THOSE!

WELL, LET'S GO TO SLEEP.
I'LL GET THE LIGHT.
GOOD NIGHT!

...THE NIGHT BEFORE A TRIP, I ALWAYS GET SO EXCITED THAT I CAN'T SLEEP.
FU FU!
IT'S STILL ONE WEEK AWAY, THOUGH.

DO YOU THINK I'LL BE OKAY WITHOUT SLEEP FOR SIX DAYS!?
I DON'T THINK I CAN SLEEP!
YOU'RE TOO EXCITED!!

IT'S AN EARLY MORNING TOMORROW

ROOOCK-A-BYE
BAAABY...
ON THE
TREETOOOP...
SHINOBU SINGING
A LULLABY FOR
ALICE

WELL, WE'RE OFF.
OKAY! HAVE A SAFE TRIP.

GET SOME SLEEP ON THE BULLET TRAIN.
AH!
NO! I DON'T WANT TO MISS A SINGLE SECOND OF THIS TRIP!
I'M PRE-PARED TO STAY AWAKE THE ENTIRE TIME!

DON'T FORGET MY SOU-VENIRS.
WOBBLE
WOBBLE
'KAY...
UH, YOU SEEM AWFULLY SLEEPY. YOU GONNA BE OKAY?

SLEEP-DEPRIVED

ALICE... KIDS WHO DON'T SLEEP SHRINK.
NO WAY!?
IF YOU SHRINK ANY SMALLER, YOU'LL DISAPPEAR ENTIRELY.
TOO BAD...
PLEASE SLEEP, ALICE!!

YAAAY!
I'M THE GROUP LEADER. EVERYONE, STICK WITH ME SO YOU DON'T GET LOST!
ROGER THAT!
YAY!
KAREN-CHAN, YOU'RE WITH US!
GROUP 3

IT'S GOING TO BE A LONG RIDE.
ON THE BUS, AND SO ON.
CHATTING AND ENJOYING THE SIGHTS ON THE WAY THERE IS HALF THE FUN OF A TRIP, RIGHT?

OH YEAH.
IF ANYONE STARTS TO FEEL SICK, LET ME KNOW RIGHT AWAY!
AYA-CHAN SEEMS MORE DEPENDABLE THAN USUAL TODAY.

SOME DOZEN MIN-UTES LATER
SENSEI... I FEEL SICK...
プルプル
QUIVER QUIVER
YOU OKAY, GIRL?
NEVER MIND, SHE'S THE SAME OLD AYA-CHAN...!

THE BEST WAY TO BEAT MOTION SICKNESS IS TO SLEEP IT OFF.
ZZZ...
I'LL TRY...
ALICE IS SLEEPING ANYWAY...
THEN...
I'LL TAKE A LITTLE NAP TOO.

ALICE-CHAN'S GROUP IS AROUND HERE, RIGHT?
CAME TO HANG OUT
AH!
I FIND THEM. OVER THERE!

すやぁ
DOZE
HUH...?

THEY GOT TIRED AND FALL ASLEEP.
LET'S PLAY CARDS.
ALREADY!?
IT'S THE FIRST DAY!!

KAREN'S GROUP
HRRM...
OLD MAID
STARE
DON'T STARE AT ME SO MUCH!

I AM READING YOUR MIND!
STARE
EEP!
YEAH, HONOKA IS EASY TO READ.

EEK! SHE'S NEVER LOOKED AT ME THIS CLOSELY BEFORE, SO MY HEART IS POUNDING!
I'M IN AWE!!
IF SHE LOOKS ANY LONGER, I MIGHT HAVE A HEART ATTACK...

I LOSE!!
WHOOSH
HEY!
THIS NOT STARING CONTEST!!

NARA PARK
WE'RE FINALLY HERE!

SO THIS IS KYOTO'S FAMOUS NARA PARK?
WOW...!
SHINO, ARE YOU KIDDING ME!?
THIS IS NARA!

THERE ARE SO MANY DEER, JUST LIKE I'VE SEEN IN PHOTOS!
WOW!!
IT'S LIKE A PETTING ZOO.

D'YOU THINK THEY HAVE, LIKE, GOATS AND SHEEP TOO!?
I WANNA SEE 'EM!
YOUKO, ARE YOU KIDDING ME!?
GOATS...

NARA PARK HAS SO MANY DEER...
... BECAUSE THE DEER ARE MES-SENGERS OF THE GODS.

LEGEND HAS IT THAT A GOD ARRIVED FOR A KASUGA SHRINE FESTIVAL RIDING A WHITE DEER.
I GIVE YOU DEER CRACKER!
SO DEER ARE SACRED!

BY THE WAY, THIS GOD WAS CALLED "TAKEMIKA-ZUCHI-NO-MIKOTO," AND—
わら CROWD
わら CROWD
AAAH! ALICE!!

SHE'S LIKE A GIRL OF THE ALPS! ♥
IS THIS REALLY THE TIME!?
WHAAAT!?

CLASS A, GATHER OVER HERE!!

I CAN'T GET A SECOND TO RELAX... I DIDN'T KNOW LEADING CLASS TRIPS WAS SO DEMAND-ING!
わた HUSTLE
わた BUSTLE
AH!
KUZE-HASHI-SEN-SEI!

I JUST REALIZED WHILE WE WERE ON THE BUS...
...YOU'D MAKE A GOOD BUS TOUR GUIDE!!!

THAT DOESN'T MATTER! PLEASE DO YOUR JOB!!
I CAN SEE IT!
RIGHT?

THE TEMPLE OF KOFUKU-JI HAS MANY BUDDHIST STATUES, STARTING WITH ASURA!
EACH OF ASURA'S THREE FACES HAS A DIFFERENT MEANING...
WOW...
THIS ASURA GUY SOUNDS A LITTLE LIKE AYA...
じーっ
STARE
OH HOLY AYAYA!
WH—
WHA—
!?
WHAT IS THAT SUPPOSED TO MEAN!?

HMPH!
AW, IT'S A COMPLIMENT!
HERE! I'LL GIVE YOU THE CHARM I JUST BOUGHT, SO CHEER UP!

SHINE
SHE DID CHANGE EXPRESSIONS THREE TIMES!
THE MEANING'S DIFFERENT!

LOOK, KAREN-CHAN! IT'S THE NARA DAIBUTSU!
"WOW!"
HE LOOK SUPER-STRONG!!

YES, STRONG ENOUGH TO PROTECT PEACE IN NARA.
HUH?
AT NIGHT, THIS GREAT BUDDHA...
...SOARS THROUGH NARA SKIES ON PATROL.
VERY COOL...
OH, WOW!
IS THAT TRUE!?
HEY, NOW...
OF COURSE YOU'D KNOW, KAREN-CHAN!

THE PILOT IS MY PAPA, AND...
GASP
Oh, I see...
TOURIST FROM ABROAD
だだだっ
TMP
TMP
TMP

HANG IN THERE...
H-HUH? OKAY...
CUT THAT OUT, KAREN!!
A LOOK OF EMPATHY!?
BONK

THIS TEMPLE IS NIGATSUDO.
THEY PERFORM A TRADITIONAL WATER-DRAWING CEREMONY HERE.
OH!
"OHH!"
KASUGA SHRINE WAS BUILT TO HOUSE ANCIENT NARA'S GUARDIAN DEITIES.
HOW BEAUTIFUL!
"BEAUTIFUL!"
THIS IS THE MEOTO DAIKOKUSHA, A SHRINE FOR MARRIED COUPLES.
EEEEK!
HEART-SHAPED WISH PLAQUES! SO CUTE!!
"PRETTY!"
AND THEN OVER HERE WE HAVE...
"OH YEAH!"
"EXOTIC JAPAN!!"
IT SHOULD BE THE OTHER WAY AROUND!

HEY, IS THAT ISA-NEE'S CAMERA?
YES!
SHE ASKED ME TO TAKE LOTS OF PHOTOS.

I TOOK THESE ONES AT KASUGA SHRINE.
OH YEAH?
SHOW US!

THE CONTRAST OF THE RED AND GOLD CAME OUT BEAUTIFULLY.
THERE'S NOTHING BUT BLOND HAIR!!

WHAT A WASTE! LET ME HANDLE THE PHOTOGRAPHY!
COME ON!
B—
BLOND HAIR, A WASTE ...!?

SIGHT-SEEING: OVER
PITCH-DARK
ARE WE IN NARA NOW? OR KYOTO...?
TONIGHT, WE'RE STAYING AT AN INN IN KYOTO!

OMIGOSH! A JAPANESE-STYLE ROOM!
IT'S TOTALLY DIFFERENT FROM SHINO'S ROOM, EVEN THOUGH IT'S THE SAME COUNTRY!

THIS IS THE FIRST DAY I'VE FELT SO IMMERSED IN JAPANESE CULTURE SINCE COMING TO JAPAN!
SNIFFLE
CLASS TRIPS ARE "EXCELLENT"!!

SORRY I'M SO WESTERN...♥
BLUSH
KEEP IT TO YOURSELF!
WHY ARE YOU BLUSHING!?

DINNER WAS DELICIOUS!
WASN'T IT?
BAM
"HEY, ALICE!!"

DO YOU HAVE PLAN FOR INDEPENDENT RESEARCH TOMORROW!?
OBVIOUSLY! WHAT ABOUT YOU, KAREN?
OF COURSE!

OH MY. IT'S EXACTLY THE SAME AS WHERE WE'RE GOING!
WHAT A COINCIDENCE!
OH REALLYYY? THEN WE ALL CAN LOOK AROUND TOGETHER. (MONOTONE)
!

WAAAAH!
KAREN...! YOU BIG SCHEMER!!
WE'LL ALL BE TOGETHER!
IF YOU THOUGHT YOU COULD HOG SHINO, YOU VERY WRONG, ALICE!

YOU KNOW YOU'RE HAPPY TOO, ALICE.
IS THIS TRUE!?

WHAT'S THE MATTER? ANXIOUS ABOUT TOMORROW?
NO...
I'M ANXIOUS ABOUT MY SLEEPING FACE...
OHHH, THAT.

IT'S FINE! YOU ONLY OPENED YOUR EYES FOR AN INSTANT.
IT'S NOT FINE AT ALL!!
IN THAT CASE...

...I GIVE YOU CUSTOM KAREN EYE MASK!
YOU DON'T MIND!?
WAAH!
NOW I MATCH KAREN'S EYES!!
YOU SURE SEEM HAPPY...

NOW, THEN...
...CLASS TRIP NIGHTS MEAN...
...STAYING UP TO GOSSIP ABOUT LOVE!

YOU ONLY GET TO DO THAT AT TIMES LIKE THIS.
HEY, ARE YOU GIRLS AWAKE...?

......
......

すや
SNOOOZE
......
THEY'RE ASLEEP.

DAY 2 OF THE CLASS TRIP IS INDEPENDENT RESEARCH DAY.
A MAIKO DRESS-UP EXPERIENCE IS TOTALLY KYOTO.
URGH...
HAKAMA ARE HARD TO WEAR TOO...
SAMURAI
HISTORICAL "WESTERN" FASHION
SORRY FOR WAAAIT.
WHITE MAKEUP
WIG
HUH?
WHUH?
WHITE!! BLACK!!

BUT ALICE AND KAREN PULL OFF EVEN KIMONOS WONDERFULLY. I CAN'T WAIT TO SEE THEM!
AND NOW WE'RE LUMPING KAREN'S GROUP IN WITH OURS...

ぞろ FILE
ぞろ FILE
OH NO! I CAN'T TELL WHO'S WHO!!
MAIKO PARADE

AH!
THAT'S AYA.
YOU LOOK GREAT!
MAYBE 'COS OF YOUR BLACK HAIR?
OF COURSE YOU CAN'T. WE'RE ALL MAIKO.
H-HUH?

TH—
THANK YOU!
YOU HAVE WHITE MAKEUP ON, BUT YOU'RE RED!!
ALICE... WHERE IS ALICE?
I'M HERE!

OH! THIS IS WHERE YOU WERE!
WHAT'S WITH THAT DOLL!? I'M OVER HERE!
SHINOBU IS CONFUSED!

I KNEW IT...SHE NOT LIKE US IF WE NOT BLOND...
SOB...
AHHHH!
WHAT HAVE I DONE!?
THEY ARE TOYING WITH HER...
IT'S NOT TRUUUE!

↑ HONOKA

I'D ALWAYS WANTED TO TRY A MAIKO DRESS-UP EXPERIENCE TOO.
GOOD THING WE PUT IT IN THE PLAN, HUH?
I GOT TO TAKE LOTS OF PHOTOS OF ALICE AS A MAIKO.

THIS ALICE IS NICE AND NEW TOO!
I CAN APPRECIATE IT!
OH YEAH. PHOTOS ...

K—
KAREN-CHAN! UM, I'D LIKE A PHOTO...
YOU WANT PHOTO!? OKAY, LEAVE IT TO PHOTOG-RAPHER KAREN!

TH...
THANKS ...
SNAP
YOU VERY WEL-COME!

OKAY, YOU GUYS!
GROUP LEADERS
IT'S TIME TO SET OFF ON OUR WORLD HERITAGE SITE TOUR.
HAAAH...

SHINO! KAREN, YOU TOO!
WE DON'T HAVE TIME TO RELAX TODAY!
IT IS A KITTY CAT!
THE GROUP MOTTO IS "BE THERE FIVE MINUTES EARLY"!

THERE'S NO NEED TO BE IN A RUSH. KYOTO ISN'T GOING ANY-WHERE!
ほんわあ～っ
GENTLE
IT'S NOT EVERY DAY YOU GET TO BE ON A TRIP. LET'S RELAX AND ENJOY IT.
UH, NO DUH!

THAT'S A GOOD POINT!
ほわあ～っ
WARM
ALICE GOT DRAWN IN!
COME BACK TO US!!

I'D LIKE A SHOT OF KAREN AND ME TO REMEMBER THE CLASS TRIP BY.
BUT I CAN'T SEEM TO SAY IT.

I DIDN'T GET TO TAKE ONE YESTERDAY EITHER ...
NO, TODAY'S THE DAY! I HAVE TO BE BRAVE!

HOW DID YOU KNOW !?
KAREN-CHAN, KANA-CHAN'S READING MY MIND!!
WAAAH!
"WOW!"
ESPER KANA!

GO ON!
WHISPER
コンッ
NOW'S YOUR BIG CHANCE.
AWKWARD
ギクシャク
UM...
UM, KAREN-CHAN, I'D LIKE A SHO... SH... SH...

SHAMPOO! WHAT SHAMPOO DO YOU USE?
HONOKA ...!?
WHO CARE ABOUT THAT...!

I USE MY MAMA'S FAVORITE EXPENSIVE SHAMPOO!
WOW!
THAT'S JUST LIKE YOU! WHAT A LIFE!

YEAH...
THAT IS JUST LIKE YOU, HONO-KA.
I'LL TRY HARDER NEXT TIME!!
COME ON!
WE'RE STARTING AT KIYOMIZU TEMPLE!

KIYO-MIZU BALCONY
IT'S SUPPOSED TO BE ABOUT THE SAME HEIGHT AS A FOUR-STORY BUILDING.
THAT'S QUITE TALL!

COMING TO PLACES LIKE THIS MAKES ME WANT TO RECITE A HAIKU.
RATE ME, PLEASE!
!
BEING SO CLOSE TO JAPANESE CULTURE HAS SHINO TALKING LIKE A JAPANESE PERSON!

THAT GIRL CALLED ALICE, SHE IS BLOND-HAIRED AND BLUE-EYED. TRULY A PRINCESS...
..."IN" KIYOMIZU TEMPLE.
NO SEASON WORDS... AND THERE'S EVEN AN ENGLISH WORD IN THERE, BUT...

WHY IS IT... THAT MY HEART IS SO MOVED ...?
SWISH
す
10
SHE'S A GENIUS...
YOU'RE GOING TOO EASY ON HER!

NEXT UP IS JISHU SHRINE! IT HAS THESE FORTUNE-TELLING LOVE STONES...
YAK
YAK
THEY SAY THAT IF YOU CAN WALK FROM ONE STONE TO THE OTHER WITH YOUR EYES CLOSED, YOUR WISH FOR LOVE WILL COME TRUE!
YAK
A MILE A MINUTE!!
OH!
IS THAT IT?
NO! MORE TO THE LEFT!
AHH... THAT'S TOO FAR...!
OOOHHH?

HANG IN THERE, SENSEI!!
IF YOU SUCCEED, YOU MIGHT GET TO MARRY A HOLLYWOOD ACTOR!!
FRANTIC
REALLY? I'LL KEEP AT IT, THEN!
MEANDER
MEANDER

GOOD LUCK—!
WAH!
GOOD LUCK, LIKE, IN MORE WAYS THAN ONE!!

GURGLE
OOF, I'M STARVING NOW.
ME TOO.
WANT TO GO HERE FOR LUNCH?

WAH! THE PEOPLE NEXT TO US ARE SPEAKING IN KYOTO DIALECT!
IT'S LIKE, "HELLO, KYOTO," RIGHT?

DIALECTS FEEL A LITTLE BIT LIKE FOREIGN TONGUES.
I KNOW WHAT'CHA MEAN!

AREN'T WE USED TO THIS?
FOREIGN LANGUAGE

SERIOUS ANSWER

KINKAKU-JI (TEMPLE OF THE GOLDEN PAVILION)
IT'S GILDED!
IT'S ALMOST THE COLOR OF ALICE AND KAREN'S HAIR.

IT'S BEAUTIFUL, YES...
...BUT THEIR HAIR IS SOFTER, SMOOTHER, BRIGHTER...
BLOND ALLIANCE
SUCH LOVELY UNISON!

WHAT'S THE DIFFERENCE BETWEEN SHRINES AND TEMPLES AGAIN?
SHRINES ARE FOR SHINTO GODS, AND TEMPLES ARE BUDDHIST!
HONOKA! WE PRAY HERE.

GOOO!
NOW!!
IN HER MIND
HONOKA?

HERE IS MY OFFERING!
ポーイ TOSS

OH, GOD! OH, BUDDHA!

M...
M...

MAY I BE ABLE TO TAKE A PHOTO WITH KAREN-CHAN!!
ビクッ JOLT
YOU SAID THAT OUT LOUD!

TAKE TWO
K-K-K... KAREN-CHAN!
WOULD YOU TAKE A PHOTO WITH ME!?

SHIIINE
OF COURSE! I WOULD BE HAPPY TO!

SHIIINE
IT'S SO BRIGHT!

I'M BEING CALLED UP...
HONO-KAAA? COME BACK TO EARTH!

SNAP

THANKS SO MUCH! I'LL PUT IT ON OUR HOME ALTAR ...!
YOU'RE TAKING IT TOO SERIOUSLY.
KAREN! TAKE ONE WITH ME TOO!
GOLDEN HAIR AT THE TEMPLE OF THE GOLDEN PAVILION—SOUNDS LIKE IT WOULD BE LUCKY!

TOO TRUE! THEN ALICE, YOU GET IN TOO!

ME NEXT!
I'LL TAKE ONE MORE!
I'D LIKE ONE TOO, PLEASE!
THERE IS LINE !?

DINNER
DELICIOUS! RIGHT, SHINO? ♡
NOD NOD
SHINO, ARE YOU SLEEPY?
NF...
YES...
YOU TIRED FROM WALKING ALL DAY?
WE WILL FEED YOU!
WHAT'S THIS...?
I FEEL LIKE A PRINCESS LIVING IN A CASTLE...
OPEN WIDE, GRANDMA! HERE YOUR FOOD!
AHHHH...
PUSH PUSH
A NURSING HOME!!

"HOT SPRING!!"
"YEAAAH!!" Let's go~
THAT'S ENGLISH FOR ONSEN!

HONOKA! NO WONDER YOU MISSING. YOU GO IN AHEAD OF US?
BLUSH
K-KAREN-CHAN!

HOW IS THE WATER?
EH HEH HEH!
IT'S PER-FECTLY WARM!

K-KAREN! THIS IS A COLD-WATER BATH!
STEAM
STEAM
HEAT FROM HONOKA IS MAKING IT LUKEWARM!
COLD WATER
WHY!?

OH NO! BUT I DECIDED I'D ONLY GO TO A HOT SPRING WITH KAREN-CHAN AFTER I STRUCK ONE!
I FOUND IT JUST FOR YOU, KAREN-CHAN!
OH!
MY HEART'S NOT READY!

HONOKA! I'LL TEACH YOU EVERY-THING YOU NEED TO KNOW ABOUT PUBLIC BATH-ING!
CALL ME "SENSEI."
YOU'RE GONNA ACT ALL SMUG WHEN YOU'VE ONLY BEEN TO A PUBLIC BATH ONCE !?
SMIRK
AYA-CHAN-SENSEI!

THANKS A BUNCH! FOR SOME REASON, I FEEL REALLY HEART-ENED.
GLANCE
HUH!?

I'M SORRY FOR SAYING SOME-THING SO ARRO-GANT!!
H-HUH? WHAT'S COME OVER YOU NOW!?

OPEN-AIR BATHS ARE THE BEST!
WHEW!
YOU HAD BEEN WANTING TO TRY ONE FOR A WHILE.

IT WAS ACTUALLY MY DREAM TO SOAK IN ONE WITH A MONKEY.
LIKE YOU SEE IN ILLUSTRATIONS.
TOO BAD WE DON'T HAVE A MONKEY HERE.

AH!
YOUKO-CHAN, COME HERE FOR A MINUTE!
WHAT UP—?

※ YOUKO'S HAIR GOES STRAIGHT WHEN SHE WASHES IT!

YOU'RE MONKEY-LIKE. CAN YOU TRY TO SAY "OOK, OOK"?
HOW SHOULD I RESPOND TO THIS SUDDEN DISS?

NOISY OVER THERE ...
OOK, OOK, OOK!
WOW! SO CUTE!

⇧ KANA

YOU KNOW HOW HOT SPRINGS HAVE DIFFERENT EFFECTS? I WONDER WHAT THIS WATER DOES?
HONOKA, TAKE GUESS!
EH!?

DO YOU FEEL ANYTHING AFTER GETTING IN?
ERM...
H...

HAPPY?
ほわーっ
BLUSH
SPRING OF HAPPINESS!?
THAT IS SO GREAT!!

I FEEL ALIVE AGAIN.
AHHH!
EEK!
THAT'S NO FAIR!

YOU SERVED WHILE I WASN'T LOOKING!
WH—!?
HOW CAN YOU SUGGEST THAT? I DID NO SUCH THING!

OKAY! THE LOSER TREATS THE WINNER TO A MEAL!
YOU'RE ON!

ほほえまー
CHARMED
THEY SEEM JUST LIKE HIGH SCHOOL GIRLS.
THEY'RE HAVING EVEN MORE FUN THAN US ACTUAL HIGH SCHOOL GIRLS...

YAWN... I'VE HIT MY LIMIT. I'M GOING TO SLEEP.
OUT OF BATTERIES
SNUGGLE
SNUGGLE
W-W-W-WAIT!! NOT YET!!

IT'S A WASTE TO GO TO SLEEP THIS EARLY!
LET'S STAY UP AND DO A MORE... CLASS TRIP-LIKE THING!
SLAM

WHAT SHE SAID!
A CLASS TRIP CALLS FOR A PILLOW FIGHT!!
THE TRIP CAN'T END UNTIL WE'VE DONE THIS!

GEEZ, AYA.
YOU SHOULD HAVE JUST SAID YOU WANTED TO HAVE A PILLOW FIGHT.
I DON'T!!

I DON'T WANT TO PLAY SUCH A BARBARIC GAME...
LAST PERSON STANDING...
...GETS RIGHT TO ORDER US TO DO ANYTHING!
!!

READYYY ...GO!
...HUH? WHERE ARE THE PILLOWS?

ずおおおっ
FOOOM
AYAYA!?

I WIN! I'M THE KING NOW!
STRONG!
DETERMINED TO TALK LOVE

OKAY. LET'S ALL TALK ABOUT LOVE. ♪
UHHH...
KINDA PUTTIN' US ON THE SPOT. THERE'S NOT MUCH TO SAY.

KAREN, WHEN DID YOU HAVE YOUR FIRST CRUSH?
ME!?
YIKES!
SHE GOT NOMI-NATED.

MY "FIRST LOVE" WAS ALICE!
JUST KIDDING!
ME!?
HEY, NOW! TAKE IT SERIOUS-LY, OR SHE'LL BE MAD—

GO ON.
BLUSH
BLUSH
YOU'LL TAKE IT!?
WILL YOU TAKE ANYTHING?

IT'S PAST LIGHTS-OUT. MAYBE WE SHOULD GO BACK ...
バサッ
RUSTLE
IT IS OKAY! IF WE HIDE UNDER FUTON AND KEEP QUIET, WE NOT GET CAUGHT!

BESIDES, THE TEACHERS ARE SO CARRIED AWAY WITH TRIP, THEY WILL NOT CHECK VERY CLOSE...
WHO'S CARRIED AWAY?
EEK!

GO BACK TO YOUR OWN ROOM!
KUJOU-SAN, AS PUNISHMENT, YOU'RE GOING TO SLEEP IN THE TEACHERS' ROOM!
連行
HAULED AWAY
"NOOOO!!"
KAREN-CHAAAN!

ALSO, I'M GOING TO HAVE YOU HANDLE THIS DRUNKARD!
AH HA HA HA!
IT'S KAREN-SAAAN!
THAT IS TOO CARRIED AWAY!

DAY 3
THE CLASS TRIP ENDS TOMORROW, HUH?
YES, THIS IS THE LAST DAY WE CAN DO SIGHT-SEEING. LET'S MAKE THE MOST OF IT!
KYOTO TOWER

DID YOU ENJOY THE TRIP, SHINO?
OF COURSE!
DID I NOT SEEM TO...?
NO... THAT'S NOT WHY I ASK... IT'S JUST THAT YOU WANTED TO GO TO ENGLAND.

I DO WANT THAT, BUT I WANT TO IMMERSE MYSELF IN JAPANESE CULTURE FROM TIME TO TIME TOO.
SINCE MY DIET AND LIFE-STYLE ARE NORMALLY WESTERN.
SHE SAYS—WITH A 100% JAPANESE PERSON'S FACE.

ブル
TREMBLE
ブル
TREMBLE
RIGHT NOW, I WANT TO WATCH THE WORLD TRAVEL PROGRAM I RECORDED SO BADLY ...
...THAT I CAN'T STOP SHAKING...
WITH-DRAWAL SYMP-TOMS!?

BUT AS LONG AS I'M WITH YOU, ALICE...
... AND OUR FRIENDS...
...I COULD HAVE FUN ANYWHERE!

ME TOO!

WE SHOULD GO NORTH NEXT!
HOKKAIDO!
THE NORTH POLE!
I'D LIKE TO SEE AN AURORA!
YOU HAVE ZERO AGREE-MENT!!

I'M KID-DING!
NEXT TIME, WE SHOULD ALL GO ON A TRIP TO ENGLAND!
REALLY !?
CAN WE!?
KAREN AND I CAN SHOW YOU AROUND!

WHEN WE GOING?
I COULD DO NEXT WEEK...!
DON'T TALK CRAZY.
YOU SHOULD MAKE IT A GRAD-UATION TRIP, DUH.

BEFORE THAT, THOUGH ...
...WE HAVE COLLEGE ENTRANCE EXAMS...
HEH!

AYA-CHAN!
AS LONG AS WE'RE WITH OUR FRIENDS, EVEN ENTRANCE EXAMS WILL BE FUN!
I'D SAY THAT'S THINKING POSITIVE, BUT I BET THE TRIP'S THE ONLY THOUGHT IN YOUR HEAD!

FINAL DAY
ぐー…
SNOOZE

THEY WERE NOISY ON THE WAY THERE…
…BUT IT'S QUIET NOW. THEY MUST BE TIRED.
くすっ
GIGGLE

IT WAS SO MUCH FUN, WASN'T IT?
YES!

ALICE AND FRIENDS SLEPT LIKE ROCKS ON TRIP THERE TOO, THOUGH!
YOU WANT SNACK?
WHY ARE YOU THE ONLY ONE WITH ENERGY TO SPARE!?

WE'RE HOOOME!
ガチャ
KACHAK
IT'S GOOD TO BE BACK.

WEL-COME BACK!
THANKS, ISAMI…
HEY!
THESE ARE THE ONLY SOUVE-NIRS!? WHAT ABOUT MY LIST!?

THAT WAS JUST TOO MUCH…
ONEE-CHAN.
OUR SOUVENIR TO YOU IS BOTH ARMS FULL OF MEMORIES!
WE BROUGHT BACK ENDLESS STORIES!
カチンッ
SNAP

ぎゃー
GRAAAH!
ぎゃー
GRAAAH!
AHHH…
YUP, WE'RE BACK TO OUR ORDINARY LIFE.

SOUVENIRS 2

AH! I JUST REMEMBERED, THERE WAS ONE MORE SOUVENIR!

IF YOU OFFER ME A STONE YOU PICKED UP IN KYOTO OR SOMETHING, I'M NOT GOING TO BE HAPPY.
RUMMAGE
RUMMAGE
IT'S NOT A STONE!

IT'S SACRED AIR FROM KIYOMIZU TEMPLE.
WHEN DID YOU DO THAT ...?

POP
SO MEAN!

I RATHER HAVE EXTRAORDINARY LIFE THAN ORDINARY LIFE!
BOO!
BOO!
ARE YOU STILL IN TRIP MODE!?

SNRRRK...
AH!
WHOOPS. I DOZED OFF.

OH, YOU. SLEEPING IN CLASS AGAIN?
シャラララ
SHA-LA-LA
BWUUUH!?

WHICH PERIOD IS IT AGAIN?
FWAAAH!
YOUKO!

BUT THAT'S WHAT'S SO CUTE ABOUT YOU.
HEE-HEE! ♥
I DON'T KNOW WHAT TO COMMENT ON FIRST—!!

WHO ARE YOU?
THE WORLD IS ON THE VERGE OF DESTRUCTION, MERU!
I'M MAGICAL GIRL AYAYA, HERE TO SAVE THE WORLD, YUP! ☆
EEEEEP!
YOU'RE MIXING GENRES, AND YOUR SPEECH QUIRK CHANGED!

WHAT'S WRONG, YOUKO!? YOU'RE NOT ACTING LIKE YOURSELF!
AYAYA'S WORRIED!
YOU STOLE THE WORDS RIGHT OUTTA MY MOUTH!

BUT I LOVE THAT ABOUT YOU TOO.
SQUEEZE
SCARY, SCARY, SCARY! THIS IS JUST SCARY!

CLATTER
I'M SORRY FOR SLEEPING IN CLASS !!
MURMUR

DING
DONG
DANG
FOR CRYING OUT LOUD, WHAT ARE YOU THINKING !?

I HAD A NIGHT-MARE...
YOU DESERVED IT, FOR SLEEPING IN CLASS...
WHAT ON EARTH DID YOU SEE IN IT?
YOU...
ME!?

BADUM
BADUM
I... I WAS IN YOUR DREAMS?
YEAH...
AND LIKE...

QUIVER
QUIVER
THE WAY YOU WERE SO HONEST AND CHEERFUL SCARED THE HECK OUTTA ME!
SHOCK

YOUKO!
THAT IS RUDE TO HONEST, CHEERFUL AYAYA!

THAT AYAYA DOES NOT EXIST ON THIS WORLD LINE, THOUGH...
THAT'S RUDE!
I DO TOO EXIST!
UH, WHAT IS A WORLD LINE?

SHE'S TALKING ABOUT A PARALLEL WORLD.
THERE ARE OTHER WORLDS THAT EXIST ON LINES PARALLEL TO OUR REALITY.

WHAT HAPPENED TO YOU, SHINO? YOU SOUND SMART FOR ONCE!
WHOA...
KAREN TAUGHT ME ABOUT IT.
THAT'S OBVIOUSLY JUST FROM SOME ANIME OR MOVIE!! IT'S USELESS TRIVIA!!

GOOD-NESS, YOUKO-CHAN. PAY MORE ATTENTION IN CLASS.
SMUG
SMUG
YEAH...I OUGHTA TAKE A PAGE OUT OF YOUR BOOK...
OOMIYA-SAAAN.

OOMIYA-SAN!
YOU'RE THE ONLY ONE WHO NEEDS TO RETAKE THAT RECENT QUIZ!

SO COME BACK TO THE CLASS-ROOM, SWEETIE!
WE'LL DO IT IN CLASS B.
DRAG
DRAG
AH...
AH...

SOMEONE, PLEASE TAKE ME TO A WORLD WITHOUT RETAKES!!
WE'LL WAIT UNTIL YOU'RE DONE!

I IMAGINE UP HYPOTHETICAL SCENARIOS ALL THE TIME.
IMAGINE? MORE LIKE FANTASIZE.

FOR INSTANCE, WHAT IF ON THE WAY TO SCHOOL ONE MORNING...
GREAT WEATHER WE'RE HAVING TODAY!
EVERYTHING IS OFF!

...I BUMP INTO SOMEONE AT A CORNER, AND THEY TURN OUT TO BE A PRINCE?
CHAOS!

IT'D BE NICE IF THERE WERE A WORLD LIKE THAT.
ARE YOU SURE!?

WHAT WOULD HAVE HAPPENED IF IT WAS ME WHO WENT ON THAT HOMESTAY INSTEAD OF SHINO?

HEYA!
THESE ARE MY TWO FRIENDS IN JAPAN!

THEIR NAMES ARE SHINOBU AND ALICE.
SHINOBU...?
“JAPANESE KOKESHI GIRL...”

I'M GOING TO JAPAN TO SEE SHINOBU...!
ROAR
HUH!? THE END RESULT IS THE SAME!!

NEXT, WHAT IF YOU ARE CASTAWAY ON AN UN-INHABITED ISLAND?
WHAT, ARE WE DOING IMPROV NOW!?

WHAT YOU TAKE IF YOU CAN ONLY TAKE ONE THING WITH YOU?
I KNOW!
ALICE.

SHINO.
THEN WE'LL LIVE ON THE ISLAND.
ARE YOU ALLOWED TO TAKE A PERSON !?

THEN I'D TAKE YOUKO AND MAKE HER TEST FOR POISON.
TEST WHAT!?

OKAY, IF WE WERE RPG PARTY...
RPG?
?
A ROLE-PLAYING GAME.

I AM HERO. YOUKO IS BANDIT.
AYAYA IS MAGICIAN. ALICE IS FAIRY.
OHH!
YEAH, I CAN SEE THAT!
REALLY?
I'M NOT A PER-SON !?

WHAT ABOUT SHINO?
SHINO IS AT THE VILLAGE ENTRANCE ...

SHE IS VILLAGER WHO SAY, "WELCOME TO OUR VILLAGE."
SHE'S AN NPC!!

SHINO WOULD BE A PRINCESS !!

SHE WOULD LET DOWN HER LONG, BLACK HAIR FROM THE TOP OF A TOWER AS A LADDER.
SO A BLACK-HAIRED RAPUNZEL ?
※ SHINOBU

THE PEOPLE INVITED INTO THE TOWER WOULD ALL BE CAPTIVATED BY SHINO.
IT'S A HORROR STORY!

I FEEL LIKE I KEEP HEARING MY NAME ...
KEEP AT IT!
YOUR FRIENDS ARE WAITING FOR YOU, OOMIYA-SAN!

BUT YOU KNOW, IF SHINO HAD NEVER MET ALICE...
...KAREN WOULDN'T HAVE COME TO OUR SCHOOL EITHER.

THEN IF I HADN'T TRANS-FERRED HERE IN MIDDLE SCHOOL EITHER...
...WE WOULDN'T BE THE GIRLS WE ARE NOW...

THAT COULD BE PRETTY INTERESTING !
OFFHANDED
I WOULD BE ME NO MATTER WHAT WORLD LINE I ON.

WAAAAAH!
NO!!
I WANT US ALL TO BE TOGETHER!!
AYAYA IS THROW-ING A TAN-TRUM!

BUT, Y'KNOW ...
...I FEEL LIKE WE'D STILL HAVE BECOME FRIENDS LATER DOWN THE LINE.
YEAH!

AYA.
KAREN.

ALICE.
AND ME...

HUH?
FEELS LIKE WE'RE MISSING SOME-ONE...
THANKS FOR WAITING!
DID YOU MISS ME?
ガラッ
SLIDE

WAH! IT'S RAINING!
ザァーーーッ
SSS
I BROUGHT UMBREL-LAS.

DO YOU HAVE ONE, AYA?
I KNOW I PUT A FOLDING UMBRELLA IN MY BAG ...

JOIN ME, LITTLE LADY?
!

I DIDN'T PARTICU-LARLY WANT TO BE UNDER YOUR UMBRELLA, FYI!
SHE CHANGED WORLD LINE HER-SELF!

ZSSSH
OH YEAH...
I WANTED TO GIVE YOU SOME-THING.
HUH?
OOH, WHAT IS IT!?
FOOD!?

DIDN'T YOU SAY IT'S SCARY IF I'M HONEST?
HOLDING A GRUDGE

BOING
WHAT ARE YOU DOING!?
OH...
IT JUST FELT RIGHT.

NICE, A CHARM!

YOU GAVE ME ONE ON THE CLASS TRIP, SO...
...I'M GIVING YOU ONE BACK.
I MISSED THE CHANCE BEFORE.
THANKS A BUNCH!

WHY A BUSINESS SUCCESS CHARM, THOUGH?
HUH!?
I GOT THE WRONG ONE!
I MEANT TO GIVE HER A GOOD GRADES CHARM!

IT'S—
IT'S FOR...IN CASE YOU START A BUSINESS ONE DAY...
ENOUGH WITH THE ALTERNATE UNIVERSES!

ガチャ
CLICK

OH?

AH!
HEY, ISA-NEE!
WE CAME OVER!
WELCOME, GIRLS.
YOU'RE LOOKING AS CHUMMY AS EVER.

...?

WHAT IS THAT POSE? PRETTY COOL.
THANK YOU VERY MUCH!

IT IS MY ISAMI IMPRESSION!!
I'VE NEVER HELD A POSE LIKE THAT.

ISAMI-SAN...
HAAAH!
AS ALWAYS, YOU WERE JUST TOO BEAUTIFUL THIS MONTH—A SIGHT FOR SORE EYES!

ESPECIALLY THIS PAGE... IT'S GODLY!
OH, MY GODDESS!
GREAT MOUNTAIN SAGE!!
EEEEK!!
WOW...
YOU'RE REALLY WORSHIPPING ME.

I APPRECIATE IT, BUT I'M EMBARRASSED HERE.
HOW COULD I NOT BE...?
TO AYA-CHAN AND KAREN...
...YOU'RE A ROLE MODEL.

ISA-NEE, IS THERE ANYBODY YOU LOOK UP TO?
HMM?
LIKE, SOMEBODY WHO INFLUENCED YOU TO BECOME A MODEL?

THERE ARE PLENTY OF MODELS I LOOK UP TO.
BUT I DIDN'T BECOME A MODEL BECAUSE I SET OUT TO DO IT...
YOU WERE SCOUTED FOR IT, RIGHT?

HMMMM...
ROLE MODELS...
...HMM?
SHE'S LOST IN THOUGHT.
SHE KINDA LOOKS LIKE SHINO WHEN SHE'S THINKIN'.
EH!?
ARE YOU SAYING I'M BEAUTIFUL!?
UH...
NOT QUITE...
WHAT DOES THAT MEAN!?
WHAT DO I LIKE, ANYWAY?

ISAMI, WOULDN'T YOU RATHER HAVE THE OTHER ONE?
IT'S FINE. SHINOBU SAYS SHE WANTS IT.
THIS ONE'S CUTE TOO.
WAAAAH!!
I DON'T WANT A CURSED DOLL! I WANT THAT ONE!!
BWAAAH!
IT'S NOT CURSED.
OKAY.
WE'LL SWITCH.

I GET THE FEELING THAT I WAS NEVER PASSIONATE ABOUT ANYTHING SINCE I WAS LITTLE.
THIS PROGRAM LOOKS FUN!
WHAT CHANNEL IS IT?
BUT WATCHING SHINO WAS FUN...
...SO LOOKING AFTER HER BECAME A SORT OF HOBBY FOR ME.
FOREIGN CASTLES ARE SO COOL!
YOU LIKE OTHER COUNTRIES, DON'T YOU?

OH, ISAMI. YOU REALLY LOVE YOUR LITTLE SISTER, DON'T YOU?

A HOMESTAY?
IN ENGLAND? ALONE?
MM-HM, AT THE HOUSE OF A FRIEND OF MINE.
YOU KNOW HOW EAGER SHINOBU GETS ABOUT WHAT SHE LIKES.
!?
NO, I MEAN...
...IS SHE GOING TO BE OKAY!? I HAVE NOTHING BUT CONCERNS HERE!
LOOK, SHE'S ALREADY SPACING OUT!!
YOU'RE WORRYING TOO MUCH!
SHE WAS JUST FINE WHEN WE SENT HER TO GRANDMOTHER'S HOUSE LAST YEAR, WASN'T SHE?
IT'S LIKE THEY SAY—IF YOU LOVE SOMEONE, SET THEM FREE. ☆
ISN'T SENDING HER ABROAD A STEP TOO FAR!?

I'LL BE OKAY, ONEE-CHAN!
"I'LL BE BACK!"
ぐっ
JAB
......
......

I'M OFF, "MY FAMILY"!
Depa
ぶん
WAVE
ぶん
WAVE
WHILE SHINOBU WAS OFF ON HER TRIP...
...I DIDN'T FEEL ALIVE.

Y'KNOW, YOU TOTALLY LOSE YOUR COOL WHEN IT COMES TO SHINO.
キィーコ
CREAK
キィーコ
CREAK
そわ
PACE
そわ
PACE
I DO NOT!

SAFETY ALARM
LIKE THAT TIME.

I DO NOT HAVE A SISTER COMPLEX!
ANYBODY WITH SHINOBU FOR A LITTLE SISTER WOULD END UP LIKE THIS.
I WONDER...
I GET WHAT YOU MEAN, THOUGH.
C'MON, YOU DON'T HAFTA BE SO WORRIED.
SHE'LL COME HOME JUST FINE.
THAT'S PART OF IT, BUT IT'S NOT WHAT I'M REALLY WORRIED ABOUT...
THINK ABOUT IT...SHE WENT ABROAD TO THE LAND OF HER DREAMS...
...BUT WHAT IF IT'S SO DIFFERENT THAN WHAT SHE IMAGINED...
...THAT SHE'S ALL BUMMED OUT WHEN SHE GETS HOME? WHAT WILL I DO THEN?
PFF!
YOU REEEALLY LOVE SHINO, DON'CHA, ISA-NEE?
!

SHINO'S GONNA BE FINE!
HECK, SHE MIGHT EVEN COME BACK AS AN ENGLISH PERSON!
Hello~
I WOULDN'T LIKE THAT EITHER!

I'M BACK!

WELCOME BACK!

CONTRARY TO MY FEARS...
...MY LITTLE SISTER CAME HOME WITH A MUCH DEEPER LOVE OF FOREIGN COUNTRIES THAN SHE HAD BEFORE.
BLOND HAIR
ENGLAND
BLOND HAIR!
BLOND HAIR!
ONE, TWO!
ONE, TWO!
I ♥ WORLD
YEAH...
SHE DOES HAVE A ONE-TRACK MIND FOR WHAT SHE LIKES...
I'D LIKE TO SEND A LETTER OVERSEAS!
OH, REALLY...?
THAT'S COOL.
IT'S AIRMAIL!
BY AIR MAIL PAR AVION
I'M A LITTLE ENVIOUS.

I'D LIKE TO TRY PUTTING ALL I'VE GOT INTO SOMETHING TOO.
HAVE YOU DECIDED WHAT CLUB TO JOIN?
HMM...
I'M NOT SURE WHAT TO DO.
ISAMI, YOU'RE SO COMPOSED FOR SOMEONE SO YOUNG.
WHAT'S THAT MEAN?
AND YOU SOUND LIKE AN OLD MAN PUTTING IT THAT WAY, MINATO.
ISAMI.
YOU REALLY LIKE THAT MAGAZINE, DON'CHA?
DO I?
WELL, YOU READ IT EVERY MONTH!
PLUS, YOU ALWAYS WANT TO PHOTOGRAPH EVERYTHING.
HUH. NOW THAT YOU MENTION IT, I GUESS I DO...

I THINK THE THINGS YOU LIKE...
...ARE THE THINGS YOU JUST END UP DOING WITHOUT THINKING.
MINATO...
THAT'S ACTUALLY SOLID ADVICE.
OH?
IS THAT A COMPLI- MENT?
OH YES.

WHAT!?
A MODEL!?
CHATTER
CHATTER
THAT'S NOT LIKE YOU AT ALL!
DEAR! DEAR, DID YOU HEAR THAT!?
I ONLY SAID I WAS INTERESTED ...

ACTUALLY, IT'S TOTALLY PERFECT FOR HER, MOM! ONEE-CHAN IS REALLY GOOD...
...AT BOTH TAKING PHOTOS AND POSING FOR THEM!
I'LL BE YOUR NUMBER-ONE FAN!
I'M SUPPORTING YOU!

THANKS.

......
AREN'CHA THINKIN' TOO LONG?

AH!
SORRY. I DOZED OFF.
NO WAY!!

THEN WE WERE WAITING FOR NOTHING ...!?
MMM...
I WOULDN'T CALL HER A ROLE MODEL...

...BUT I THINK THAT SHINOBU'S MIND-SET IS INCREDIBLE, IN MORE WAYS THAN ONE.
FU FU FU!
A-ARE YOU PICKING ON ME AGAIN!?

I RESPECT YOU, HA-HA.
THAT WASN'T A COMPLIMENT, RIGHT!?

AWW!
IT'S A COMPLIMENT.
IT'S TRUE!
C'MON!

AFTERWORD

THANK YOU SO MUCH FOR PICKING UP VOLUME 7 OF *KINIRO MOSAIC*! AS I MENTIONED IN THE VOLUME 6 AFTERWORD, SHINOBU AND THE GIRLS ARE IN THEIR FINAL YEAR OF HIGH SCHOOL NOW. WHEN I BEGAN WORKING ON THIS SERIES, I DIDN'T THINK IT COULD CONTINUE THIS LONG, SO I'M TRULY GRATEFUL. WE GOT A SPECIAL ANIME EPISODE, AND I TOOK A TRIP TO ENGLAND THIS YEAR... I FEEL LIKE DRAWING *KINIRO MOSAIC* HAS BROADENED MY HORIZONS. ANYWAY, I'D LIKE TO CONTINUE WORKING HARD AT MY OWN PACE, AND I'D BE HAPPY IF WE MET AGAIN IN VOLUME 8!

Special thanks!

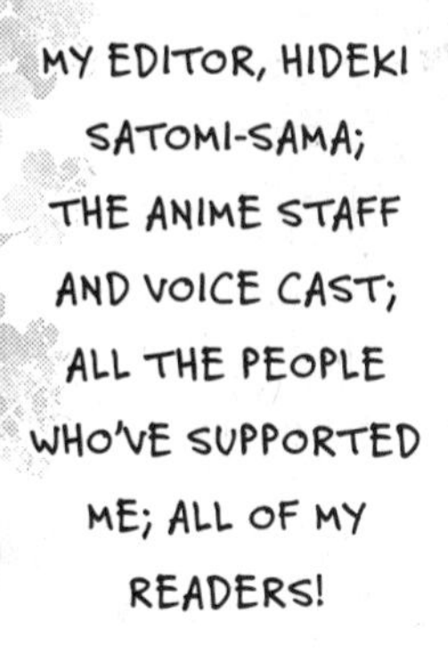

MY EDITOR, HIDEKI SATOMI-SAMA; THE ANIME STAFF AND VOICE CAST; ALL THE PEOPLE WHO'VE SUPPORTED ME; ALL OF MY READERS!

Yui Hara

ONCE UPON A TIME, IN A CERTAIN LAND, LIVED LITTLE RED RIDING HOOD.
MAN, I'M STARVING.
GURGLE
LITTLE RED RIDING HOOD.
WILL YOU TAKE CAKE AND WINE TO YOUR SICK GRAND-MOTHER FOR ME?

WHAT THE HECK IS THIS?
THAT'S WHAT YOUR GRANDMOTHER WANTS MOST OF ALL.
SHE CAN'T LIVE WITHOUT IT.
LITTLE RED YOUKO-CHAN
I DON'T WANT A GRANDMA LIKE THAT...

MEANDER
MEANDER
WATCH OUT FOR WOLVES, AND DON'T MAKE ANY PIT STOPS!
YAAAY! THE FLOWERS ARE BLOOMING!

RUSTLE
HEEEEELP!!
WHOA!
IT'S A WOLF!

WHAT'S THAT?
A BAD HUMAN CAUGHT YOUR FRIEND!?
BOO HOO!
BUT I CAN'T EXACTLY TRUST A WOLF...

NONCHALANT
I-I'M ACTUALLY A PUPPY!
OH, FOR REAL? NEVER MIND, THEN.
RED RIDING HOOD WAS EASY TO TRICK.

SHE'S OVER THERE!
BLOND HAIR...
"HELP MEEE!!"
YIKES!
I CAN'T TELL WHICH ONE IS THE WOLF!!

GRANNY, DON'T COMMIT CRIMES!!
FLING
CACLANK

SHIIINE
IT'S CLEANSING HER...
WAS IT A CURSE?

SOMEHOW OR ANOTHER, THEY ALL LIVED HAPPILY EVER AFTER.
I HADN'T TOUCHED BLOND HAIR IN SO LONG THAT MY HEALTH TOOK A TURN FOR THE WORSE...
WHAT?
THAT'S HOW YOU WERE SICK?
EH HEH HEH!
ALL'S WELL THAT ENDS WELL.

kiniro
mosaic

Translation Notes

PAGE 10
Aya is probably thinking that she and Youko would look like a couple in **matching outfits** rather than sisters, thus the blushing. It's a trendy thing to do in Japan on dates.
In anime/manga fandoms, fictional characters are sometimes referred to as **2-D** (and real people as **3-D**).

PAGE 23
Visiting a shrine a hundred times, or *ohyakudo mairi*, can be done to show the gods your sincerity when wishing for something.

PAGE 29
Sakura mochi is a pink-colored sticky rice cake (*mochi*) with a cherry tree (*sakura*) leaf pickled and wrapped around it. It is traditionally eaten in the spring only.

PAGE 34
Youko's **yumstick** (*umaabou*) is a play on *Umaibou* ("delicious stick"), a common and very cheap cylindrical puffed corn snack in Japan.

PAGE 37
The **Japanese school year** starts in April, so it coincides with Alice's birthday.

PAGE 38
Youko says she wants to do *ohanami* ("flower-viewing"), the Japanese custom of enjoying the sakura trees when they bloom in the spring, generally by **picnicking** under them.

PAGE 51
Bento are boxed lunches; care is often taken to make them look nice. The lunch Youko gives Aya is called a *hinomaru* ("rising sun/Japanese flag boxed") bento—it's just rice with a pickled plum in the center to represent the sun on the Japanese flag. It's as simple as lunches get.

PAGE 53
The proverb Shinobu and Karen want to say is *sannin yoreba monju no chie* (literally "three people together have the wisdom of Manjushri," which is equivalent to "two heads are better than one"), but they're getting mixed up at the mon part. Youko's guess, ***monjayaki***, is a variety of *okonomiyaki* (a savory pancake whose ingredients you choose as you like).

PAGE 55
A teacher drawing a **flower** on your schoolwork is like getting a gold star.

PAGE 57
Osechi, the **New Year's food box**, is a multi-tiered stack of boxes (much like a *bento* box) containing special, symbolic dishes eaten for New Year's.

PAGE 60

The city of **Nara** is the capital of Nara Prefecture, and borders Kyoto Prefecture. It was the first permanent capital of Japan (from 710–784) and has several major sightseeing locations. The city of **Kyoto**, capital of Kyoto Prefecture, was also a historical capital of Japan (from 794–1869) and is considered a cultural center of the country.

PAGE 61

Translated as **What happens in Kyoto stays in Kyoto**, Karen's proverb in Japanese is *tabi no haji wa kakisute* ("throw away your sense of shame while traveling").

PAGE 67

Are bananas candy? is a common question associated with field trips because schools often decide how much a student is allowed to spend on treats for a trip. If bananas aren't considered candy, then the students won't have to worry as much about hitting their spending limit.

PAGE 71

Nara Park, established in 1880, is in Nara, not Kyoto! Both Shinobu and Youko should know better...One of the oldest parks in Japan, Nara Park is famous for its more than a thousand free-roaming deer and spans over a thousand acres.

PAGE 72

Kasuga Shrine is famous for its lanterns and deer. The path to Kasuga Shrine goes through Nara Park. Though it was established in 768, like many Japanese shrines and temples, the shrine has been rebuilt several times—it's traditional for Japanese shrines to be rebuilt regularly with the same design (often because of fire or earthquake damage).

PAGE 73

Kofuku-ji Temple, established in 669, is most famous for its five-story pagoda, the second-tallest in Japan. It's also in the Nara Park area.

The **Nara Daibutsu** is the world's largest bronze Buddha statue. It's housed in Todai-ji Temple's Great Buddha Hall and is fifteen meters tall.

PAGE 74

Nigatsu-do ("Hall of the Second Month") is another structure at Todai-ji, founded in 752. The **water-drawing ceremony** (*omizutori*) is performed to cleanse people of sins and usher in spring. On March 12, priests draw water from Wakasa Well underneath the hall and offer it to Buddhist deities, then to the people. It's said that water only springs from the well on that day.

Meoto Daikokusha is a sub-shrine of Kasuga Shrine. The shrine's deities are a married couple (*meoto* means "married couple"), so it's popular with couples who want a happy marriage.

PAGE 77

Maiko are apprentice *geisha* (traditional female entertainers/hostesses). Shinobu is dressed as a *haikara-san* (*haikara* coming from "high collar"), which was a word for someone who followed new, more **Western** fashions in dress and lifestyle as Japan was modernizing. The word came into popular use around 1898, during the Meiji period.

Hakama are traditional Japanese bottoms that can have legs—like pants—or be open, like skirts. Shinobu is wearing a women's *hakama*, which is rare, as *hakama* are typically worn by men.

PAGE 80

Kiyomizu-dera is a Buddhist temple founded in 778. *Kiyomizu* means "clear water," and its name comes from a waterfall inside the temple complex. The girls are looking out from the temple's famous hillside balcony, which features prominently in the Japanese expression: "to jump from the balcony at Kiyomizu," which is used in the sense of "to take the plunge."

PAGE 81

Jishu Shrine, located inside the Kiyomizu complex, is Kyoto's oldest shrine for gods of love and matchmaking.

PAGE 82
Ginkaku-ji ("Temple of the Silver Pavilion") is a Zen Buddhist temple that was originally built as a place of rest for shogun Ashikaga Yoshimasa (1436–1490). It was to be covered in silver foil, thus the name, but was left incomplete upon Yoshimasa's death.

Nijo Castle, completed in 1626, was a residence of the Tokugawa shoguns.

Kinkaku-ji ("Temple of the Golden Pavilion"), completed in 1397, was a villa bought by shogun Ashikaga Yoshimitsu and turned into a Zen temple upon his death. The pavilion is coated in gold-leaf gilding, giving it a striking look. Ginkaku-ji is actually based off of Kinkaku-ji (Yoshimitsu was Yoshimasa's grandfather).

PAGE 84
A **home altar** (*kamidana*) is a miniature shrine set up above eye level on a wall in one's home, containing Shinto-related items. One might pray at the home altar or offer food or flowers.

PAGE 87
There is a park called Jigokudani Monkey Park in Nagano, where monkeys famously bathe in the hot springs in the winter.

PAGE 90
Kyoto Tower is the tallest structure in Kyoto at 131 meters, with a hotel and stores at its bottom and an observation deck 100 meters up. Its construction was completed in 1964.

PAGE 91
Hokkaido is the northernmost prefecture of Japan, known for its cold climate and swaths of undisturbed forest. It's considered Japan's last frontier.

PAGE 96
It's common for mascot characters in magical girl anime to have a **speech quirk**—generally, adding special "cute" sentence endings to the tail ends of their statements (like Aya's *meru*, which doesn't mean anything but sounds cute).

PAGE 99
Translated as **improv**, in Japanese, Youko says that their discussion is getting to be like an *oogiri*—a *rakugo* comedy contest in which a host poses a question to his fellow *rakugo* storytellers, and they compete to give funny or witty answers. Karen is dressed like a *rakugo* storyteller in panel one.

HE
BREAKS
HEARTS,
NOT
DEADLINES!
MONTHLY GIRLS'
NOZAKI-KUN
IN STORES NOW!
Yen Press
YenPress.com
Monthly Girls' Nozaki-kun © Izumi Tsubaki / SQUARE ENIX

PRESENTING THE LATEST SERIES FROM

JUN MOCHIZUKI

THE CASE STUDY OF VANITAS

READ THE CHAPTERS AT
THE SAME TIME AS JAPAN!

AVAILABLE NOW WORLDWIDE
WHEREVER E-BOOKS ARE SOLD!

www.yenpress.com

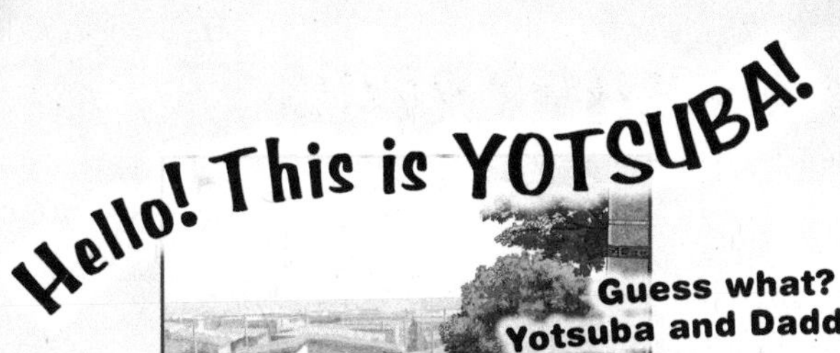

Guess what? Guess what?
Yotsuba and Daddy just moved here from waaaay over there!

!

And Yotsuba met these nice people next door and made new friends to play with!

The pretty one took Yotsuba on a bike ride!
(Whoooa! There was a big hill!)

And Ena's a good drawer!
(Almost as good as Yotsuba!)

And their mom always gives Yotsuba ice cream!
(Yummy!)

And...
And...
OHHHH!

kiniro 7 mosaic

Yui Hara

Translation: Amanda Haley
Lettering: Rochelle Gancio

Yen Press
1290 Avenue of the Americas
New York, NY 10104

Visit us at yenpress.com
facebook.com/yenpress
twitter.com/yenpress
yenpress.tumblr.com
instagram.com/yenpress

First Yen Press Edition: September 2018

Yen Press is an imprint of Yen Press, LLC.
The Yen Press name and logo are trademarks of Yen Press, LLC.

The publisher is not responsible for websites (or their content) that are not owned by the publisher.

Library of Congress Control Number: 2016946069

ISBNs: 978-1-9753-0177-4 (paperback)
978-1-9753-0234-4 (ebook)

10 9 8 7 6 5 4 3 2 1

WOR

Printed in the United States of America